Presenting Patti

Susan Saunders

AN
APPLE
PAPERBACK

SCHOLASTIC INC.
New York Toronto London Auckland Sydney

No part of this publication may be reproduced in whole or in part, or stored in a retrieval system, or transmitted in any form or by any means, electronic, mechanical, photocopying, recording, or otherwise, without written permission of the publisher. For information regarding permission, write to Scholastic Inc., 730 Broadway, New York, NY 10003.

ISBN 0-590-44354-2

Copyright © 1991 by Daniel Weiss Associates, Inc. All rights reserved. Published by Scholastic Inc. APPLE PAPERBACKS is a registered trademark of Scholastic Inc. SLEEPOVER FRIENDS is a registered trademark of Daniel Weiss Associates, Inc.

12 11 10 9 8 7 6 5 4 3 2 1   1 2 3 4 5 6/9

Printed in the U.S.A.   28

First Scholastic printing, May 1991

Chapter
1

I had no idea what I would be getting into that Friday afternoon when Mrs. Mead told us about the conference.

"Anyone from the fifth through eighth grades may attend," she said. "It will take place next Friday through Monday, at Montvale College, which is about two hours from here. All you need to do is get your parents' permission, and there will be a small fee to cover the costs of the conference." Mrs. Mead smiled at us. "I hope several of you will decide to go. It will be a perfect opportunity to get to know other students your age from all across the state."

Stephanie Green turned around in her seat in the first row and winked at me. I tried not to laugh.

Trust Stephanie to turn a boring-sounding conference into a boy-watching event!

Henry Larkin raised his hand. "You said it's a leadership conference. Does that mean we're going to study presidents and stuff?" he asked. "Is it going to be like a big history class?"

"No, not at all," said Mrs. Mead. "You'll learn how to be better leaders yourselves in today's society." She glanced at the paper she was holding. " 'The purpose of the conference is to teach you how to interact with your peers in a constructive manner,' " she read out loud.

Stephanie turned around and winked at me again.

"Stephanie, is there something in the back of the room that I should know about?" Mrs. Mead asked.

"Uh, no," Stephanie said. "The, uh, conference sounds very interesting."

This time I bit my lip to keep from laughing.

"Yeah, right," Henry whispered to me. We sit next to each other. I really like Henry. What I mean is, for a boy, he's not bad. "Sounds like a total yawn," he said softly.

I shrugged my shoulders. I don't know — maybe it would be fun to meet other kids from all over the state. But if we had to sit through a bunch of boring lectures, I'd rather spend the weekend at home with my friends. I knew one thing for sure: If they weren't going, I wasn't either! We do almost everything together.

"We" are Stephanie, Lauren Hunter, Kate Beekman, and me, Patti Jenkins. We're all in 5B with Mrs. Mead at Riverhurst Elementary. Lauren and Kate sit way in front of me in the second row, and I could see them passing notes to each other about the conference. Stephanie sits in front of them, in the first row. I'm stuck in the back row — well, not exactly stuck, because I *do* get to sit next to Henry.

It seems like the four of us have been best friends forever. But actually, only Kate and Lauren have known each other since they were little kids. They grew up practically next door to each other, and have been doing stuff together since kindergarten. They started the tradition of our Friday night sleepovers. Lauren's dad used to call them the "Sleepover Twins," but they don't look anything alike. Lauren has brown hair and she's tall, while Kate is short with blonde hair. Their personalities are total opposites, too. Lauren is as messy as Kate is neat. Sometimes I wonder how they get along, but they do! Mostly they just tease each other a lot.

Stephanie moved to Riverhurst in the fourth grade and became friends with Lauren right away. It took a little longer for her to win Kate over, but she did. Stephanie and Kate tend to argue about things, but it's only because they're so much alike. They're both a little on the bossy side. (Actually, they can be downright pushy, but I won't go into that now.) Stephanie has black curly hair, and almost always wears red, black, or white clothes, or any combination of those colors. It makes her easy to spot in a crowd, even though she's short.

Sometimes I wish *I* were short, but I'm not. I'm the tallest girl in fifth grade — and I'm taller than most of the boys, too! It's humiliating. My mom says they'll catch up soon, but it can't be soon enough for me. On the plus side, I like being able to play sports like basketball and volleyball. I have brown hair, I'm skinny, and I have a little brother named Horace and a cat named Adelaide.

"Over the weekend I'd like each of you to write a short essay describing what you think the most important qualities are for a leader," Mrs. Mead went on. She handed out sheets describing the conference.

"The conference organizers are holding a competition, and anyone who would like to may enter his or her paper. It should be three pages long," Mrs.

Mead said. Just then the bell rang, and everyone started scrambling for the door. "And write neatly!" Mrs. Mead added in a loud voice. "I'm used to your handwriting, but the judges won't be. And don't forget to bring in your signed permission slips!"

"I can't wait to go to the conference!" we heard Jenny Carlin say from across the room. "I just know my parents will say yes."

"If that's the kind of person we have to 'interact' with," Lauren said, "count me out!"

I had to agree. Jenny can be pretty obnoxious when she wants to be. If we had to spend a weekend with *her*, boring lectures would be the least of our problems.

"There are going to be hundreds of kids at this thing," said Kate, shaking her head. "We won't even see her."

Lauren held out a pen and a notebook. "Can I get that in writing?"

"Just trust me," Kate said. "This conference will be a lot of fun."

"I agree," said Stephanie. "Just think of all the kids we'll get to meet. I'm definitely going."

I looked at Lauren and shrugged. It's always a surprise when Kate and Stephanie agree about something right off the bat. "Maybe they're right," I said to Lauren as we walked down the hall.

She didn't look convinced. "And maybe we'll have the most boring weekend of our entire *lives*," she said.

"We can talk about it tonight at the sleepover," Stephanie said, throwing open the school's front door. "Last one to the bikes has to kiss Wayne Miller!" she cried.

Considering that Wayne Miller is the grossest boy in our class, for once I was glad I had long legs!

Lauren tore open a bag of tortilla chips and sat down on the floor. We were spread out in my attic. There's not much up there except a bunch of boxes and old trunks. It's the perfect place to tell ghost stories because there's only one light, and it can be pretty dark and creepy. We use it for sleepovers at my house sometimes because my bedroom is so small, and that night there were five of us.

"Hope, can you pass me the dip?" Lauren asked.

"Sure." Hope Lenski passed a small container to her. Hope moved to Riverhurst a little while ago, and already we're pretty good friends. She doesn't come to all of our sleepovers, but since the sleepover was at my house that night, I'd decided to invite her. I know her a little better than the others do because we're both in the Quarks at school, a club for kids who really like science. She's in 5B with us, too.

"What happened to your health kick?" Kate asked Lauren. Lauren has a huge appetite, and Kate's always teasing her about it. Lately, though, ever since we'd started hanging out with Hope (and Lauren had had *three* cavities!), Lauren has been eating carrot sticks and rice cakes instead of cookies and chips. Hope is a vegetarian and she's incredibly healthy.

"These tortilla chips are blue," said Lauren. "They're organically grown. The dip is made with vegetables and yogurt — no sour cream."

Stephanie rolled her eyes. "Okay, but how does it taste?"

"Try it," said Hope.

Stephanie stuck the edge of a chip into the dip and carefully crunched it. "Not bad," she said. "Pass me some more!"

"What do you want to do tonight?" I asked everybody.

"How about Truth or Dare?" said Stephanie. Truth or Dare is one of our favorite sleepover activities.

"Okay," I said. "Who wants to go first?"

"I will," said Kate, taking charge as always. "Lauren, truth or dare?"

Lauren took a sip of soda. "I'm probably going to regret this, but I'll take the dare."

Kate rubbed her hands together. "I want you to call Royce Mason and ask him if he's going to the leadership conference."

"Me? Why should I call him? You're the one who likes him!" Lauren protested.

"That's exactly why I shouldn't call him," Kate said smugly.

"Now he's going to think *I* like him," Lauren complained.

"Disguise your voice," Stephanie suggested. "And while you're at it, call Taylor Sprouse and see if he's going, too."

"Hey — only one dare at a time," Lauren protested.

"It sounds like you two have already decided you're going to the conference," I said.

"Sure, why not?" said Kate. "It sounds like fun."

"Of course Kate has to go," Lauren joked. "Next year the conference will probably be *named* after her!"

Kate shrugged. "I can't help it if I'm a born leader."

"And modest, too!" Hope laughed.

8

"What about you, Hope? Are you going?" I asked.

"I can't. My mom is coming to visit next weekend," she said.

"You're kidding! That's great," I told her. Hope's parents were divorced a few months ago, and she lives with her father. Mrs. Lenski lives all the way out in California, and Hope hardly ever gets to see her.

Hope nodded. "I can't wait."

"Too bad you have to miss the trip," Stephanie said. "I'm going, for sure."

"Now, why are you going. . . . It couldn't be the fact that we'll get to meet boys from all across the state, could it?" Lauren wondered out loud.

Stephanie giggled and threw a pillow at her.

"Lauren, are you going, too?" I asked.

"Well, I didn't want to, at first. Then I looked at the schedule — do you realize that we're going to miss two whole days of school if we go to this thing?" Lauren grinned. "How can I pass that up?"

"So, Patti, you're definitely coming," Kate declared. "You have to!"

"I guess I'll go," I agreed. Secretly, the thought of all those other kids made me nervous. I get really shy around people I don't know. Lauren, Kate, and Stephanie, on the other hand, would probably make a hundred new friends in the first hour.

"What do you mean, you *guess?*" Stephanie said. "This is going to be the most fantastic trip this year! We're going to be on our own — "

"With about a thousand chaperons, no doubt," Lauren added.

Stephanie waved her hand in the air. "Who cares? We'll get a room in a dorm together — it'll be like we're in college."

"It's too bad you can't come, too," I told Hope. "But I bet you'll have a great weekend here."

Hope smiled. "Thanks — it should be a lot of fun."

"Maybe she'll bring you some cool clothes from Los Angeles," Stephanie said.

"Okay, okay — let's get back to official sleep-over business," Kate said. She jumped up off the floor, reached for the cordless phone, and handed it to Lauren. "You'd better make those calls before it gets too late!"

Lauren groaned and reached for the phone book. "I'll get you for this someday," she mumbled.

Chapter
2

"Boy, I'm glad that's done!" Stephanie pulled her hair back from her face.

"Me, too," Lauren said.

We had just finished our weekly "job" at the Pizza Palace, our favorite pizza place in the mall. A few weeks ago we had convinced John, the owner, to start recycling. Since he doesn't have enough time or employees to do the job, we help him during the busy times — like Saturdays. It was all Stephanie's idea. The Pizza Palace is one of our all-time favorite places to eat, so I like to help out.

"I'm glad our parents said we could go to the conference," Kate said. "It would be horrible if one of us were left behind."

"I'm surprised your parents let you go," I said

to Stephanie. She'd gotten in trouble recently for trying to take on too many projects at once.

"No problem," she said. "I convinced them I needed a weekend away. Plus, it's for school, so they were excited about that." She tossed an empty soda can into the aluminum recycling bin. "Ready to go shopping?"

"Don't tell me — you need five new outfits for our trip," Lauren said.

Stephanie folded her arms across her chest. "No, of course not! *Four*, maybe." She started laughing.

When we got to our favorite store, Just Juniors, Stephanie said, "Oh, look! The new summer stuff is in!" She ran over to the "Latest Arrivals" rack and started plowing through the clothes.

"It's like letting a cat free in a fish store," Lauren said, shaking her head.

"Didn't you want to get a new shirt?" Kate asked me.

I nodded and started looking at the rack of new clothes. I have a hard time buying clothes. I don't have a "style" like Stephanie, and I never know what to get.

"How about this?" Lauren held up a blue and white striped T-shirt.

"I don't know — it looks more like you," I told her.

"Try it on," Lauren advised.

"Try this one, too," Kate said. She handed me a pink blouse. "I think it's perfect for you."

Pink isn't really my color, but I took it anyway. Stephanie's arms were full of clothes, but she stopped on her way to the dressing room to pick out some things for me, too. "If you're going to get this shirt, you need the matching shorts, too," she said, handing them to me. Then I showed them a lime-green T-shirt with orange piping around the cuffs and neck. "I kind of like this," I said.

Stephanie shook her head. "It's last year's news," she said. "Besides, those aren't your colors."

I didn't care if it wasn't the latest fashion statement, I just liked it. I stuffed it under the other shirts and brought them into the dressing room. First I put on the blue and white striped shirt, then I tried on some of the shirts Stephanie gave me. "Come out and let us see!" Stephanie urged.

I stepped out wearing the shirt and shorts ensemble. I felt like a five-year-old.

"That looks terrific on you!" Lauren said.

I frowned at my face in the mirror.

Stephanie walked around me. "Didn't I tell you

that outfit was great? It shows off your long legs, and the bright colors really make your eyes stand out."

I took another look in the mirror. The last thing I wanted to do was show off my long legs! The colors were fun, though — bright pink, yellow, and green. "I don't know," I said. "I still have a few more things to try on." I went back and changed into the lime-green T-shirt. With my blue jeans, I thought it looked really cool.

I went back out to model it for Stephanie. "Don't you think this is better?" I asked her, smiling at my reflection in the mirror.

Stephanie was in about the twelfth outfit she had tried on so far. "It's okay," she said. "But it's not as flattering as the other shirt."

"It's practically the same colors," I pointed out.

Stephanie put her arm around my shoulders. "Trust me. You looked absolutely adorable in the matching set."

I giggled. "Stephanie, you sound like the saleslady!"

"That's what happens when you spend a third of your life shopping," Lauren teased her.

I went back into my dressing room and changed into my regular clothes. I couldn't decide what to get. Should I trust my own instincts, or Stephanie's? She *does* know a lot about clothes.

When I walked back out into the store, Stephanie was waiting for me at the cash register. She was getting a cotton sweater and a pair of pants. Kate and Lauren were already out in the mall corridor, talking to some kids from our class. I held up the two things and took another look at them. I was just about to put the shorts outfit back on the rack when Stephanie took it out of my hand.

"Great choice," she said, smiling as she put it on the counter. "You'll knock all those other fifth-graders out with this." She smoothed the shirt's collar.

I sighed and put the lime-green T-shirt back on the rack. That was one decision I didn't have to make — Stephanie had made it for me! I hoped she was right about the outfit — I wasn't really looking forward to showing the whole state my long legs.

On Monday we all brought in our permission slips and gave them to Mrs. Mead before class. "Uh-oh," Lauren whispered as Jenny Carlin handed Mrs. Mead a piece of paper. "We're going on a road trip with the Wicked Witch of Riverhurst."

15

I had to laugh. As I said, Jenny can be pretty mean. Just a couple of weeks ago, when Mrs. Mead and Mrs. Wainwright, our principal, wanted to skip me into sixth grade — and not her — she had said some pretty rotten things to me. Fortunately, my parents gave up on that idea when I convinced them I couldn't leave my class — and my friends had all signed a petition asking me to stay.

"I wonder who else is going?" Kate said.

"Well, we know Royce Mason and Taylor Sprouse aren't," Stephanie said. "Thanks to Lauren!"

Lauren blushed. "I'm not saying anything around them for six months. If they ever recognize my voice, I'll die."

The bell rang, and Mrs. Mead started class. We went through our math homework first, and I got everything right. Math is my best subject, besides science. Then Mrs. Mead asked people to read their essays in front of the class. Whenever I have to do a book report or any kind of oral presentation, I get really nervous.

"Let's do this alphabetically," Mrs. Mead suggested. "Robin, you go first."

I tried not to think about the fact that I would have to get up there, too, as I listened to everyone else read their essays.

16

Kate went second — her paper was pretty good, but it reminded me of TV commercials. It was full of phrases like, "Go for it," and, "If you do the best you can, you'll come out ahead."

Stephanie and Lauren did okay, but Mrs. Mead told Stephanie that hers was too short. They're both great at speaking in front of class, though. Lauren cracked a few jokes to open her speech — she always does it that way.

I was watching the clock closely. It was almost time for lunch. Maybe I wouldn't have to read mine after all. *Ring, bell, ring,* I chanted in my head.

No such luck. Mrs. Mead called my name, so I got up slowly and walked to the front of the room. "To me, a leader is someone who isn't afraid to stand up for what he or she believes in," I began. My voice was trembling a little, and I cleared my throat. I started reading my paper as fast as I could.

A minute or so later, I finished my essay and went back to my seat. Mrs. Mead clapped her hands together. "Excellent, Patti! I like what you did with the assignment."

"Too bad we couldn't hear it," Jenny whispered loudly to her best friend, Angela Kemp. "Talk about speed-reading!"

The bell rang — finally! — and we rushed

down the hall toward the cafeteria. "Don't listen to what Jenny said," Lauren advised me. "Your speech was great."

"Even if you did go a *little* fast," Stephanie said.

I let out a nervous laugh. "Well, I didn't want us to be late for lunch."

"You know, Patti, I think you should enter your essay in that contest," Lauren said.

I stared at her. "Why?"

"It's really good. You might win," she said.

"I'm entering mine," Kate said, grabbing a tray and starting through the line.

"Why am I not surprised?" Lauren whispered to me, and we both giggled. "Seriously, though. You might win a great prize, or money. You have nothing to lose."

"Then how come you're not entering?" I asked her. I put an apple and a carton of milk on my tray.

"You know I'm not very good at writing. And Mrs. Mead didn't call *my* paper 'excellent,' " Lauren said.

"You should do it, Patti," Stephanie said. "Who knows? You might win something really good."

"No, I don't think so," I said. I'm not really into competitions, and I wasn't sure I wanted a bunch of people I didn't know reading my essay.

"Hey, Patti," someone behind me said. I turned around and saw Jenny. "Did you ever see those ads where the guy talks really fast? Maybe you could get a job doing that." She and Angela burst out laughing.

"You should enter it and win, just to serve them right," Lauren said as we walked over to our usual table where Stephanie and Hope were already sitting.

I shook my head. "That would just give them more to tease me about."

We put our trays on the table and sat down.

Stephanie leaned closer to me and whispered, "Guess who's going to the conference?"

"Who?" I whispered back.

"Henry," she said softly. "I heard him talking about it when I walked by their table." She squeezed my arm. "Wait till he sees you in that cute outfit."

Chapter
3

"Stephanie, do you think you brought enough?" Kate pointed at the huge suitcase the bus driver was putting in the luggage compartment.

"I want to be prepared," Stephanie answered as we climbed on the bus. "Look — there are four empty seats together. Let's grab them."

I sat next to Lauren, and Kate and Stephanie sat behind us. I looked around for Henry — he was in the back with Mark Freedman, one of his best friends.

"It's too bad Hope couldn't come with us," Lauren said. "But it's a good thing some other people came along, right?" She squeezed my arm.

I could feel my face turning pink. "Yeah, I guess so," I said. Everyone had been teasing me nonstop about Henry since we danced together at the Valentine's Day party.

Karla Stamos sat down across the aisle from me. "Hi," I said.

"Hello," she replied. She's in our class, and is nice, I guess, but she's also pretty boring.

"Can you believe there are three buses just for Riverhurst Elementary?" she asked me. "I didn't know so many people wanted to go."

"I know," I said. "I guess no one minds missing school, though."

"It's not like we're missing it, really. This conference is going to be very educational," Karla said in a serious tone.

"And fun, too, I hope," I added. "I can't wait to see — "

"Hey, Patti!" Kate reached up and tapped me on the shoulder. "We need your advice about something."

I turned around in my seat. "What?" I asked.

Stephanie leaned closer. "We just wanted to rescue you," she whispered.

"From the famous Stamos Snooze Machine," Lauren added softly.

I looked at them, puzzled. Why did they think

they had to save me? I could handle myself in a conversation. If I didn't want to talk to Karla, I didn't have to. I was actually enjoying talking to her. "You don't have to worry about me," I said. "We were just making small talk."

Kate rolled her eyes. "You know Karla," she whispered. "It starts with small talk, and the next thing you know she's telling you how she skinned her knee in third grade."

"She's not that bad," I said.

Lauren, Stephanie, and Kate looked at me as if I were crazy.

The bus ride lasted about two hours. At one point we passed one of the other buses, and we tried to look inside and find out who else was going to the conference. Unfortunately, the only people we recognized were Jenny Carlin and her sidekick, Angela, and a few seats behind them, Ginger Kinkaid and Christy Soames, two girls from 5C who we don't get along with either. Actually, Christy is okay when she's by herself, but when she's with Ginger, they're as bad as Jenny and Angela. Ginger's the kind of person who's only nice to you if she can get something out of you — and Jenny's not even *that* nice! I told myself we'd have to keep our distance from all four of them once we got to the college, or else the weekend wouldn't be any fun.

We got there around four o'clock. The college was already on summer vacation, so the campus was pretty empty. It was beautiful, with lots of old brick buildings and huge green lawns. We stopped in front of the student union and piled out of the bus.

"We'll register here," announced Mrs. Mead. "Then you'll bring your things to your dormitories. We'll meet again at dinner tonight."

"Wow! I can't believe how many people are here," Lauren commented as we stepped through the front doors of the student union.

"I know — there must be a thousand kids, at least," Kate said.

"And I see one I want to know already." Stephanie craned her neck to watch a boy walking into the student union snack bar.

Kate hit her on the arm. "Don't be so obvious!"

"I think this is our line," I said, pointing to the sign that read STUDENTS A – L. I was glad we all got to wait in the same line. I didn't want to get separated from my friends in such a big crowd.

They were handing out large packets of information, including a schedule and tickets for meals at the cafeteria. When I got to the front of the line and said my name, the woman behind the desk smiled. "So *you're* Patti Jenkins!" she said.

"Uh . . . yes," I answered.

"Here's your packet," she said, grinning from ear to ear. "But before you do anything else, you're to meet with the conference director, Roseanne Hayes."

"Me?" I asked. "Patti Jenkins — are you sure you have the name right?"

"Mm-hm," she said, still smiling. "Ms. Hayes is over there." She pointed to a small table. "Go ahead."

"Am I in trouble?" I asked. "I sent in the fee and — "

"What's going on?" Lauren asked me.

"I'm supposed to meet with Ms. Hayes, the director of this thing," I told her.

Lauren shrugged. "Maybe it's good news. I'll go with you, okay? For moral support."

"Thanks," I said. "That lady probably confused me with another Patti Jenkins from somewhere else, anyway." I couldn't imagine why Ms. Hayes would want to meet with me — I had just gotten there!

"Hi, my name is Lauren Hunter, and this is Patti Jenkins," Lauren said boldly when we got to the director's table.

"Patti! How nice to meet you!" Ms. Hayes beamed at me. "I enjoyed reading your essay so much, and, I'm happy to say, so did the other judges. Congratulations! We judged your essay one of the four best."

I just stared at her with my mouth hanging open. *My* essay? How had it gotten from my notebook in Riverhurst — to here? Had I sleepwalked to the mailbox, or what?

"Are you sure you have the right person?" I asked.

"Of course!" Ms. Hayes said. "Isn't this your essay?" She handed me a folder.

I quickly opened it and looked at the paper inside. There it was, my essay. "But how — "

"I can't believe it — that's terrific," Lauren interrupted me, throwing her arm around my shoulder. "You deserve it!"

Suddenly I remembered how Lauren had tried to convince me to enter my paper in the contest on Monday. Then, after lunch, she had asked to look at it because she thought it was so good. . . . Come to think of it, I never had asked for it back.

"Lauren, did you — " I began.

"So what does she win?" Lauren asked, interrupting me. "What's the grand prize?"

"Well, seeing as how this weekend will teach you all how to be better leaders, we thought the *best* prize would be for the contest winners to show everyone what wonderful leaders they already are!" Ms. Hayes said happily. "And that's why the four best papers will be a part of the opening ceremony tomorrow morning. And you, Patti, will go first!"

I felt my stomach quake — and it wasn't from hunger, either. "Do you mean we have to read our essays to *everyone*?" I asked.

"I certainly do!" Ms. Hayes said. "And I just know everyone is going to be so impressed when they see what a mature and intelligent fifth-grader you are, Patti." She grinned at me and walked away.

I couldn't believe Lauren had gone behind my back like that. I knew she only meant well . . . but still, it was *my* paper. And she should have found out about the big "prize" first. Some prize! It was going to be torture! Pure torture!

"Patti, are you all right?" Lauren asked me.

"Oh, um, sure," I said.

"You looked like you were on another planet for a second," Lauren said nervously.

I wish I were, I thought. "Lauren, I can't get up in front of all those people!"

"Sure you can," Lauren said as we walked back

to Kate and Stephanie. "I'll help you. You know I wouldn't have done it if I didn't think you deserved to win," she said.

I didn't say anything. How could I be mad at Lauren? She was only trying to help me. But I felt mad, anyway.

When we told Kate and Stephanie what happened, they were both excited for me. "This is great!" Stephanie said. "Our best friend is a celebrity!"

I cringed. That was the *last* thing I wanted to be.

"I knew this conference was going to be fun," Kate said. "I wish I could read my essay, too."

"You can read yours instead of me," I said. "I won't mind."

Kate shook her head. "No, you won — you get to read it."

"Did you look at your room assignment yet?" Stephanie asked. "Kate and I are in the same room, in Clark Hall — room 314." The four of us had requested a suite together, but we weren't sure we would get one.

I opened my packet — I hadn't even had a chance to look at it yet. "I'm in 314, too," I said.

"So am I!" Lauren cried. "This is going to be great! A Friday night sleepover in our very own dorm room."

I couldn't believe it, but I almost wished Lauren weren't in the same room with us. I didn't like feeling angry toward anyone — I never do. But I felt as though she had really messed things up for me. Now I wouldn't be able to have any fun. At least not until my dumb speech was over.

"I asked the lady at the desk how to get to Clark Hall — we just go down that sidewalk over there," Stephanie said.

"How are you going to carry your trunk — I mean, suitcase?" Lauren teased her.

Stephanie held up a strap. "It has wheels, silly."

We walked out the doors and headed toward our dorm. Four or five buses were parked outside, and dozens of students were streaming into the student union to register.

"I can't get over how many kids are here, can you?" Lauren asked me.

I gave her a half-smile. That was the problem. There were way too many kids! If I had been nervous about reading my essay in front of the class, how was I going to do it in front of a *thousand* people?

Chapter
4

"Here it is — 314. Thanks," Stephanie told the boy who had carried her suitcase up three flights of stairs. "I really appreciate it."

"Yeah, sure," he said. He turned and dashed back down the stairs.

"Wasn't he just the cutest?" Stephanie said.

"You were practically batting your eyelashes at him," Kate said. "You know we could have carried it."

"Sure, but why?" Stephanie laughed.

Lauren opened the door and we stepped into our suite.

"This dorm is pretty nice," Kate commented as we walked into the living room. "I mean, it's not the Plaza, but — what are you two doing here?"

Jenny and Angela were sprawled on either end of the couch.

"This is *our* room," Jenny replied. "What are *you* doing here?"

"*We're* supposed to be here," Stephanie answered. "Room 314. *You* must be in the wrong dorm."

Jenny shook her head. "Nope. One of the workshop leaders brought us here."

"This is like a bad dream," Lauren whispered.

That was exactly what I was thinking! I walked around the suite. There was a bathroom with two sinks and two showers, and there were two bedrooms — with four beds in each one. "I think this suite is for eight people," I told everyone.

"Then you guys have one bedroom, and we have the other all to ourselves," Jenny said.

"I don't think so," a voice said in back of us.

We all turned around and saw Ginger standing in the doorway. Christy was behind her, struggling to hold her suitcase. She's a real clothes nut, too, like Stephanie. As usual, she and Ginger were dressed almost exactly alike, in designer jeans and neon T-shirts.

"This is *our* room," Ginger said. She looked at

30

Jenny and then at Kate. "*You* must have the wrong dorm."

"I wish," Kate said. She checked her registration packet again. "They wouldn't have put us in the same room — they couldn't have."

"But they did," said Jenny, showing her room assignment to Ginger.

Ginger frowned. "How do they expect us to live in these conditions?"

"You got me," Stephanie said, crossing her arms in front of her chest.

"Never mind a bad dream — this is a nightmare," Lauren said softly.

Christy dragged her suitcase into the suite. "Which room is ours?" she asked.

Jenny frowned and gestured to the one on the left. "We already put our stuff on *our* beds," she said pointedly.

"Unbelievable," Ginger muttered. She gave a little huff and she and Christy walked into their bedroom.

"Let's bring our stuff into the other room," I said. I didn't want to get caught in the middle of a fight between Ginger and Jenny. It was bad enough we were suitemates!

Stephanie dropped her suitcase on a bed. "Maybe we can switch to another suite," she suggested glumly.

"All the dorms are full," Lauren said, shaking her head. "I heard someone say that at registration."

"Well, we have our own bedroom, at least," Stephanie said. "Maybe if we try really hard, we'll forget they're in the other one."

Just then Jenny let out a loud shriek of laughter. She has the most obnoxious laugh of anyone I've ever heard — except maybe Ginger!

"And . . . maybe not," Stephanie said.

"Let's go down to dinner," Kate said. "At least we won't have to sit at the same table with them."

"I knew I should have packed my earplugs," Lauren joked as we walked through the living room.

"This is going to be a very long weekend," Stephanie said as we shut the door behind us.

"You're not kidding," I mumbled. It was definitely off to a horrible start!

Dinner wasn't too exciting — or too edible, either. I guess that's one thing that doesn't change as you get older. College food tastes just as lousy as elementary school food. I wasn't hungry, anyway. I kept looking around at all the people in the dining hall. Every single one of them was going to be at the opening ceremony tomorrow, listening to *me*. What made it even worse was that Ms. Hayes came over to our table and told me how much she was looking forward to my speech. She said I could add anything I wanted to my paper, and that I could ad-lib if I wanted to. That means I could make remarks that popped into my head while I was up there.

I had a few ideas for ad-libs. How about, "Thank you very much, good-bye," or, "I don't want to read this, sorry." I knew that wasn't what she had in mind, though.

When we got back to the suite, our roommates were nowhere in sight, thank goodness.

"You know, I don't even feel safe in the same room with those creeps," Stephanie said. "They'll probably go through all our stuff and ruin it."

"I don't think so," Lauren said. She peered into their bedroom. They had left a sign on one of the beds that said NO TRESPASSING! STAY OUT! THIS MEANS YOU!

"Get real," Stephanie said. "Like we even want to get near their room!"

We all walked into our bedroom and looked around.

"I'm sleeping here," Stephanie said, pulling her

suitcase off the bed. "I like to be near the window."

"Me, too," Kate said, flopping onto the other bed near the window.

I was just about to grab the bed in the corner when Lauren said, "I'll take this bed. I like to sleep facing the wall." She chose the one in the corner.

That left me with the bed closest to the door. I didn't want to complain, but it was definitely going to be the noisiest place to sleep. And I needed a good night's rest — I had a big day ahead of me. I wasn't about to kick anyone out of their bed, but it made me kind of angry the way everyone had chosen ahead of me, as if I didn't even matter.

"Is something wrong, Patti?" Lauren asked me.

"No," I said. "Not really." I opened my duffel and got out my toothbrush.

"Thinking about your speech tomorrow?" Kate asked.

"Yeah," I admitted. "I keep trying not to, but it isn't working."

Stephanie jumped up from her bed. "I have an idea. Why don't you let me fix your hair tomorrow morning?"

I wrinkled my nose. "I don't know. Maybe."

"Tell you what — we can help you get ready," Kate said.

"That's a great idea!" Lauren said. "And the first thing you need to do is eat something. You hardly ate any dinner. You need to keep your strength up, you know." She took a tin of sugar-free oatmeal-raisin cookies from her overnight bag.

"Patti, let's decide what you're going to wear tomorrow. I think that's the most important thing," Stephanie said.

Kate shook her head. "The most important thing is how Patti presents herself. I'm going to teach her everything I know about public speaking."

"We only have a couple of hours," I reminded everyone. I wanted to be ready and everything, but they were acting as if I were in the Miss America pageant!

"Okay," Kate said as she got up and started pacing around the room. "Let me see your paper for a second. Then we'll work on how you're going to present it."

"I'm just going to read it," I said, handing it to her.

"Yeah, Kate, lighten up — she's not going to act it out!" Lauren said, giggling.

Stephanie walked over to me. "Show me the clothes you brought, and I'll put your outfit together." I put my clothes on the bed and she rummaged through them. Finally she pulled out my short beige skirt (it's the only miniskirt I own, and she's the one who gave it to me) and my new T-shirt. "This is it!" she cried. "Perfect!"

I looked at her and raised one eyebrow. "I was thinking of wearing my blue pleated pants with the red short-sleeved sweater," I said. Get up on stage in a miniskirt? No way!

"Do you want to look incredibly chic, or do you want to look plain and ordinary?" Stephanie asked me.

"Well . . ."

"Lauren, what do you think? Isn't this a great outfit?" Stephanie held up the T-shirt and skirt. "It goes even better with the skirt than the matching shorts. And she has these beige flats that go perfectly."

Lauren nodded. "That looks nice."

"Then it's settled." Stephanie tossed my clothes onto the bed and grabbed a cookie.

"Patti, come over here," Kate instructed me. I walked over to her. "Stand right here. Okay, now we'll sit over there, and you pretend we're the audience. I want to see your delivery."

"The only delivery I want to see is a pizza," said Lauren. She and Stephanie started laughing.

36

"Do I have to?" I asked Kate. "You guys don't really want to hear this again."

"Practice makes perfect!" Kate chimed.

In that case, I should probably stay up *all night* practicing, I thought.

"Come on," Kate urged me. "We won't make fun of you."

I took a deep breath. "Leadership," I began. "To me, a leader is someone who isn't afraid — "

"Wait a second," Kate interrupted. "You have to say your name first. It's the proper thing to do when you make a speech. Say, 'Hello, my name is Patti Jenkins, and this is my essay on leadership.' "

I held out the paper to her. "Why don't you say it? No one will ever know it's not me."

"Except Ms. Hayes," Lauren reminded me. "And Mrs. Mead, and Henry, and Mark and — "

"Stop!" I cried. "Don't remind me."

"Okay, we don't have much time," Kate said. "Start from the beginning."

I let out a loud sigh. "Hello, my name is Patti — "

"The Pinhead!" someone added.

I looked up and saw Christy and Ginger standing in the doorway.

37

"This looks like a fun way to spend a Friday night," Ginger commented. "Doesn't it, Christy? I mean we always sit around and give speeches to each other." She cackled with laughter.

"What's so funny?" asked Jenny, coming into the room with Angela.

"They're listening to Patti talk," Ginger said, still laughing. "Isn't that fascinating?"

Lauren stood up and put her hands on her hips. "It just so happens that we are listening to the best essay writer in the whole state! And you will be, too, tomorrow morning, when Patti reads it in front of everyone."

Jenny looked surprised. "You won the leadership essay contest?"

I nodded and looked at the floor. *Here it comes,* I said to myself.

"Well, I just hope they pass out copies of the essay — otherwise no one will be able to understand what you're saying!" Jenny quipped. The other three started laughing.

"Oh, go soak your heads," Stephanie told them.

"Yeah." Kate went over to the door. "And get out of *our* room!" They stepped back and she shut the door in their faces.

"Don't listen to Jenny or Ginger. They're just

jealous," Lauren told me. "You'll do great tomorrow."

"I don't want to practice anymore," I said. "I think I'm ready." That was a lie, but I didn't want to hear about, think about, or talk about my speech any longer! It would be horrible, no matter what. The only consolation was that in twelve hours, it would be over and I could start having fun again.

"Let's get ready for bed and then we can listen to the new Boodles tape," Stephanie said. "I brought my tape player."

"So there's something besides clothes in that suitcase!" Lauren said.

I brushed my teeth, washed my face, and got into my nightgown. It was hard to ignore our roommates, but we managed to. Back in our room, Stephanie was dancing around to the new tape. Lauren and Kate were writing postcards to send to their parents. I just lay down on my bed and stared at the ceiling.

Two hours later, when they had turned out the lights and fallen asleep, I was still staring at the ceiling. I could hear Jenny's shrieking laugh through the closed door. I turned over about a thousand times, but I couldn't get comfortable. And our suitemates were still awake at three A.M. I know, because I kept looking at my watch, counting the hours until morning.

I knew my eyes were going to be all puffy the next day. It would be a miracle if I could even *see* my speech, never mind read it!

Chapter
5

I rolled over and put my pillow over my ears. Jenny and the others were *still* making noise! It sounded as if they were in the bathroom. I sneaked a glance at my watch. It was seven-thirty — I must have fallen asleep some time after four o'clock. Since the opening ceremony wasn't until nine o'clock, I closed my eyes and tried to fall back to sleep.

A few seconds later I heard Stephanie yell, "I said, get out of the shower already!"

"Hey — who used my toothpaste?" Kate shouted.

I sat up in bed and rubbed my eyes. Jenny and Ginger weren't the only ones who could make a lot of noise!

"I didn't use your stupid toothpaste," Ginger

41

yelled above the noise of the shower. "I brought my own!"

"Then how come the cap on mine is missing?" Kate demanded.

"Maybe you swallowed it by mistake — I don't know!" Ginger answered.

At the rate they were going, the whole dorm would be awake in no time. Stephanie and Kate stormed back into the room. Stephanie had a towel slung over her shoulder, and Kate was waving her tube of toothpaste in the air.

"Can you believe them?" Kate said. "What nerve!"

"Ginger's been in the shower for half an hour," Stephanie complained. "I hope she turns into a prune!"

Kate examined her toothpaste. "I know one of them used this — last night this little squeeze mark wasn't here."

"Oh, hi, Patti," Stephanie said, sinking onto her bed. "We didn't know you were up."

I wasn't, I felt like saying. "Actually, I, um, just woke up a few minutes ago. Where's Lauren?" I asked.

"Down in the cafeteria, where else?" Stephanie replied. "She was hungry."

"You know what, Stephanie?" Kate tapped her bare foot against the floor. "We should do something about the Bathroom Hogs. We have rights, too."

"You're right," Stephanie said. "Let's report them to our floor counselor."

"For starters," Kate agreed. "After that, we might have to take matters into our own hands!"

I stood up and went to get my clothes out of my duffel.

"If you're looking for your outfit, I already put it in the bathroom," Stephanie informed me.

"In the bathroom?" I repeated sleepily.

"The steam will get rid of the wrinkles," Stephanie said. "We want to make sure you look your best today!"

"Thanks," I said, trying to smile. Wrinkles were the least of my worries. "Are you sure that skirt doesn't make my legs look too long?"

"There's no such thing as legs that are too long for women," said Stephanie. "I read that in *Teen Topics*."

"But we're not women," I said.

"Same thing!" Stephanie scoffed. "We're close, anyway."

I wasn't so sure about that. I opened our bedroom door and listened in the hallway. "Sounds like one of the showers is off," I said, picking up my towel from the dresser.

"Finally!" Stephanie flew past me and ran into the bathroom. The swinging door practically hit me in the face as it closed.

Too bad, I thought. If it had knocked me out, then I definitely wouldn't have had to give my speech.

"Here you go — the special Speechmaker's Breakfast!" Lauren whipped the napkin off her arm and laid it down on the desk next to my bed. "A blueberry muffin, scrambled eggs, and Canadian bacon," she said, producing a plate from behind her back. "And some orange juice, too!" She took a small carton out of her jacket pocket.

I just stared at the food. It was really nice of Lauren to bring me breakfast. I knew she was trying to make up for getting me into this mess in the first place. But I couldn't eat a thing. Some people say they get butterflies in their stomachs when they're nervous — not mine. Mine feels like someone's playing the bongo drums on it instead.

I smiled weakly at Lauren. "Thanks. I can't eat, though. I'm too nervous."

"Don't be!" Kate told me. "You're going to be great."

"Just pretend that we're the only ones in the audience," Stephanie suggested. "You're not nervous in front of us, are you?"

"No," I said. "I guess not."

"We'll be in the front row — just look at us when you get up there," Lauren said.

"I guess we should get going," Kate said. "The guest of honor can't be late."

"Are you sure you don't want any breakfast?" Lauren asked.

I nodded.

"Okay, then." She grabbed the muffin. "Let's go!"

I took one last look at myself in the mirror. My hair had turned out pretty well, despite the fact that by the time Stephanie got out of the shower there was no hot water left. My eyes were a little red, but I hoped no one would notice.

"Don't worry — you look fantastic," Stephanie said with a grin. We headed out of our room and down the hall.

When we got to the auditorium, my knees started shaking — not a great thing to do when you're

45

wearing a short skirt, let me tell you. Five or six adults — teachers, I guessed — were sitting on the stage. Ms. Hayes had told me I was to sit in the front row along with the other contest winners, but that my friends could join me if I wanted moral support. Did I!

We walked down to the front row. Ms. Hayes was up on stage and she waved at me. I was sliding into my seat when Henry jumped into the chair next to mine.

"What are you doing here?" I asked him.

"It's nice to see you, too," he joked. He settled back in his seat as if he was trying to get comfortable.

"I mean, what are you doing in the front row? You hate the front row," I reminded him. "You never sit there."

Henry shrugged. "I can sit here if I want to," he said.

"This thing is going to be so boring." I shook my head.

Henry turned to me and grinned. "Someone I know is giving a very interesting speech."

I felt all the color drain out of my face. "Really? Who?" I managed to gasp.

Henry hit me lightly on the arm. "Don't play dumb. Lauren told me you won the essay contest. I think it's great. Too bad you don't get any cash, though."

I gritted my teeth and cast a sideward glance at Lauren. Great! Just great! Now the first person I'd see when I went up to read my speech would be Henry, in the front row.

Ms. Hayes stepped up to the microphone. "Good morning, boys and girls! Welcome to the twelfth annual leadership skills conference! I'd like to begin with some general comments about the concepts we'll explore this weekend."

I heard someone behind me whisper, "I had to get up early for this?"

Ms. Hayes went on for about ten minutes. While she talked, I glanced at Lauren again. She was calmly listening to the speech. Meanwhile, my stomach was doing somersaults as I waited for my name to be called so I could get up and embarrass myself in front of everyone! That didn't seem fair. I had told her I didn't want to enter the contest, but she hadn't listened to me. She'd gone ahead and entered *my* essay just because *she* thought it would be fun.

Maybe instead of a leadership conference, we should be at a friendship conference, I thought. "A friend is someone who listens to you," my speech would start. "A friend doesn't push you into doing something you don't want to do. A friend doesn't enter your essay in a contest and then tell the boy you like to sit in the front row and watch you sweat!''

I felt Stephanie shaking my arm. "Go on, Patti," she whispered. "Didn't you hear her call your name?"

Everyone in the auditorium was clapping. I took a deep breath, stood up, and walked toward the steps. It seemed like it took me about an hour to get up on stage. Ms. Hayes shook my hand and adjusted the microphone to my height.

I put my paper down on the podium. I had been gripping it so tightly that it was all curled up, and it fell onto the floor. I knelt down and tried to pick it up gracefully. Talk about embarrassing!

I smoothed out my speech and faced the audience. I looked at the front row, just like Lauren had told me to do. Kate gave me the "okay" sign with her thumb and forefinger. Lauren was making a goofy face. Stephanie just winked at me. I couldn't even look at Henry.

It's now or never, I told myself. *Just go slow, and take it easy.* My mouth was so dry, I could hardly talk.

"Hi," I said. "My name is Patti Jenkins, and this is my, uh, my — '' Then everything went black!

Chapter
6

"Patti! Wake up!"

"Patti, are you all right?"

I opened my eyes. For some reason, Kate, Stephanie, and Lauren were leaning over me. They looked fuzzy, though. "Is it time to get up?" I asked them.

They gave each other worried glances.

"Patti, we're at the opening meeting," Kate said, taking my hand. "You fainted."

I sat up as fast as I could, even though it made me feel sick. I couldn't believe it. I was lying on the stage — in front of everyone! I could hear kids whispering and talking to each other. I closed my eyes again. "Please tell me this isn't happening."

"Do you feel okay?" Stephanie asked. "Did you hit your head when you fell?"

"I don't know," I said. "I don't remember."

Ms. Hayes and the other teachers were leaning over me, too.

"It must be one of those twenty-four-hour bugs," Ms. Hayes said sympathetically.

"Are you all right, dear?" one of the others asked me.

"I think so," I said. If I didn't die from humiliation, I *might* survive.

Lauren reached down and took my arm. "Kate, get her other side," she said. "You'll feel better once you're back in your seat, Patti."

"After you get your strength back, promise me you'll go to the infirmary and see the campus nurse," Ms. Hayes told me. "Just in case."

"I'll take her," Lauren offered.

I got to my feet, and Lauren and Kate helped me off the stage. I didn't look up once. I didn't want to see everyone laughing at me. It was horrible.

"Are you okay?" Henry asked when I sat down.

I nodded and kept staring at the floor.

"Unfortunately, Patti is not feeling well today," Ms. Hayes announced to the crowd. "But, being the true leader that she is, she was brave enough to try to read her speech anyway. Let's give her a big hand."

Everyone started applauding, and I slunk down in my seat as far as I could.

"I told you you'd do great," Henry whispered. "You didn't even have to say anything, and they liked you!"

I looked at him out of the corner of my eye. He was smiling at me. Sure, it was funny to *him*. *He* hadn't passed out!

"I'm glad there's nothing wrong with you," Lauren said when we left the infirmary. "If you had to go home, it would be terrible."

Not really, I thought. In fact, it would be wonderful! Then I would never have to see anyone again.

"So did the nurse tell you to take it easy?" Lauren asked. "Personally, I think you should eat a big lunch. Maybe if you'd had some breakfast you wouldn't have fainted."

I thought of all the kids who would be in the dining hall. "Actually, I'm still not very hungry," I said.

"Do you want to go back to the room and lie down? I can bring you some food later," Lauren suggested. "You know what? I think it's a cookout. It should be pretty good. They can't ruin hamburgers, can they?" She laughed nervously.

I knew she was being extra-nice because she felt bad about my presentation. But it didn't help. Lauren was being a good friend to me *after* I'd looked like a fool in front of everyone. So what? She couldn't change the fact that I had fainted because I was so nervous, and all because I was reading an essay *she* had sent to the contest.

"So what do you say? Will you come to the cookout with me, or do you want to wait back at the dorm?" Lauren asked.

I didn't want her waiting on me hand and foot for the rest of the trip, so I said, "Okay, I'll go. We have to sit behind a tree, though."

"Don't be ridiculous," Lauren said. "I'm sure everyone's forgotten about that by now."

"It was only two hours ago," I reminded her.

"You know how people's memories are short!" She laughed again. "I mean, I can't even remember what we did yesterday."

"I can," I said. No one was going to forget the fifth-grade girl who passed out before she even got to her speech. In fact, I was probably going to be the number-one topic at lunch! I pulled my hair forward over my face and slouched a little so I wasn't so tall.

"Don't worry," Lauren told me as we approached the lawn in front of the dining hall. It was covered with big grills and long tables of food. "Here, wear my sunglasses. There are hundreds of kids here. No one will recognize you."

I slid the shades onto my nose and took a paper plate from the serving table. I had to eat sooner or later, and I did feel a little weak.

"Hey, are you feeling okay?" the boy in front of me in line asked. "You went down *fast*."

"I wish I had that on video," another boy said. I glared at Lauren over the top of her sunglasses. No one would recognize me, huh?

After lunch we went back to the dorm and changed into T-shirts and shorts. It felt good to get out of my miniskirt. Why had I let Stephanie convince me to wear it, anyway? From now on, whenever I looked at those clothes I was going to think of them as "The Fainting Outfit." I almost wanted to throw them out!

I was glad that our roommates weren't around while we were in the room. If I knew Jenny, she would have some comments about my speech — or lack thereof.

Our information sheets said our first workshop that afternoon was an outdoor obstacle course called

"Accepting the Challenge." I didn't feel up to accepting any challenges. If it were up to me, I would have stayed inside all afternoon and read a book. But we all had to go, like it or not.

"This is going to be great," Kate said when we walked onto the football field.

"I thought you hated sports," Stephanie said.

"Well, this isn't exactly a sport. It's more like a test of our confidence and courage," Kate said.

Lauren looked at me and rolled her eyes. "Here we go again," she mouthed.

Normally I would have laughed, but I just couldn't. My face felt like it was going to crack, I was so tense.

"I think we have to break into different groups," Kate said. "It looks like they have four courses set up."

"That group over there is ours." Stephanie grabbed Kate's arm and started pulling her across the field. Lauren and I followed.

"How do you know?" Kate asked, shaking off Stephanie's hand.

"Because," Stephanie said, nodding toward the group, "see that guy in the surf shorts, with blond hair?"

Lauren laughed. "He just has to be in our group, right?"

"Right." Stephanie smiled.

"Give me a break," Kate said, sighing.

Stephanie turned to me. "There are lots of cute guys here, don't you think?"

I just shrugged. "I guess."

"You *guess*? Look at him." She pointed to a tall boy with dark hair and wraparound sunglasses. "And him, and — "

"Patti's not looking for anyone new. She already has a boyfriend, remember?" Lauren said, grinning.

"Not anymore," I mumbled.

"What do you mean?" asked Lauren.

After the way I'd acted at the opening ceremony, I was sure Henry would never want to be seen with me again.

"Never mind," I said, shaking my head.

"Henry must be here somewhere," said Lauren. She stood on her tiptoes and surveyed the crowd.

I crossed my fingers behind my back. I hoped Henry was way across the field, so he wouldn't see me mess up on the obstacle course, too.

"Okay, people, this is what we're going to do!" a counselor's voice boomed over a megaphone.

"Each group will run through its own obstacle course. Since the purpose of this weekend is to teach you leadership skills — "

"How many times have we heard *that?*" Lauren joked. A bunch of kids around us laughed.

"One of the most important things is to learn not to be afraid of new challenges," the counselor continued. "You must learn to tackle problems — like this row of tires here — boldly. You must also find out what your limits are, and accept that there are things you may not be able to do."

Like giving speeches, I added in my head.

"This guy makes it sound like we're going into Basic Training," Stephanie said, frowning.

"Do we actually have to run through those tires?" I asked.

"I don't care about those," Stephanie said, "but look at the wall over there with the rope hanging down. I'm going to look like an idiot if I try to scale that thing."

"No problem," Kate said with a wave of her hand. "You can do it."

"Kate?" Lauren shook Kate's shoulders. "Kate, are you in there?"

Kate isn't athletic at all, so it was funny to hear her get psyched about running all over the field.

Stephanie and Lauren are pretty good at sports. I am, too, only this wasn't like playing softball back in Riverhurst. There were so many people on the field, it felt more like the Olympics!

"One last thing," the counselor said. "We want you to push yourselves, but be careful. If there's something you can't do, ask one of us for help. And remember — fear may be the biggest obstacle of all!"

"This guy *must* be from the Marines," Lauren said. "Look out, he might try to recruit you when you run by."

The other counselors were organizing the groups into lines. "Let's get near the front," Kate said.

"Let's not," said Stephanie. "Let someone else mess up first."

I watched the first few people run through the tires on the ground. It didn't look too hard, but . . . anything could happen. If I fell down *again* — well, I didn't want to think about what would happen. I'd probably win the Least Likely to Ever Become a Leader award.

A few minutes later we moved to the front of the line. "We're next," Kate said excitedly. She took off and started stepping through the tires. Stephanie followed her, running at top speed. I stepped to the side, hoping Lauren would run past me.

"Come on, Patti," she said. "It's now or never."

"How about never?" I said.

"Don't worry — you'll do great," she said.

I'd heard *that* before! But I decided it would be even more humiliating if I didn't even try. "Okay," I said, "let's go."

I ran through the tires as fast as I could, just to get it over with. I concentrated really hard so I wouldn't slip. I made it!

"Terrific!" the counselor at the end shouted. "Way to move!"

"See, I told you it would be fine," Lauren said when we finished.

We walked over to join Kate and Stephanie at the rope climb. Stephanie was staring at the wall with a worried expression. "I don't know if I can do this," she said.

"Let's skip it," I suggested. "He said we should learn our limits."

"Pfft!" Kate scoffed. "You're supposed to take the challenge, not run away from it."

Stephanie folded her arms across her chest. "Okay, then. Let's see *you* make it over that wall."

"No problem." Kate flipped her hair back out of her face and charged straight at the wooden wall.

She grabbed the rope and tried to get her feet on the wall so she could climb up it. Only her feet kept slipping, so she was just hanging onto the rope and swinging around.

"No problem, right?" Lauren shouted to her.

"What's the matter, is it too much of a challenge?" Stephanie added.

Kate dropped down to the ground, backed up, and then ran straight at the wall again. This time her feet grabbed it, and she made her way up and dropped over to the other side.

"I guess that's what we deserve," Lauren grumbled. "Well, who's next?"

"Not me," Stephanie said. She was watching the boy in the surfing shorts run through the tires. "I think I'll wait and see if he can help me over."

"Are you serious? Stephanie, you can do it by yourself," Lauren told her.

Stephanie shrugged. "Maybe. But why should I?"

"Because it's silly to ask a guy for help when — "

"Hurry up, you three! Others are waiting!" one of the counselors yelled at us.

"I don't know about this," I said, shaking my head.

"Come on, Patti! You can do it!" Kate shouted

from the other side. "Mind over matter!"

Oh, well, I thought. Deciding I'd better get it over with, I ran at the wall. For once, it was a good thing I was tall, because I started out with a high jump that put me pretty far up the wall. I made it to the top without too much trouble, when suddenly I heard a boy yell, "Don't faint!"

Would I *ever* live that down?

Chapter
7

"So did you talk to Mr. Wonderful?" Lauren asked when Stephanie sat down at the table. We were eating dinner in the dining hall, or trying to, anyway. They were serving some kind of chicken casserole that tasted like glue, so we were filling up on rolls and apple pie.

"A little," Stephanie said. She had gone over to talk to Chip, the blond boy she had met at the obstacle course.

"Where is he from?" Kate asked, buttering a roll.

"Northfield. He's in seventh grade, he plays tennis, and his favorite group is The Feds." Stephanie took a sip of milk.

"Did you ask him to help you get your dinner?" Lauren asked.

Stephanie looked puzzled. "What do you mean?"

"Well, I just thought you might need him to help you put the milk in your glass or something," Lauren said.

"No, I poured it myself," Stephanie said.

"Really?" Kate wiped her mouth with a napkin. "That's amazing."

"Yeah, we're really proud of you." Lauren reached over and patted Stephanie on the back.

"Maybe you should ask him to bring your tray up when you're done, though," Kate suggested. "You wouldn't want to strain yourself or break a nail."

"What are you talking about?" Stephanie asked innocently.

"Stephanie, you've been acting like an airhead all afternoon," Lauren pointed out.

She was right. Stephanie *had* been acting like a ditz in front of all the boys.

"I have not!" Stephanie protested.

"Oh, and I suppose you couldn't have walked on that balance beam thing by yourself," Kate said. One of the obstacles had been a long, narrow piece of wood that we had to walk on without losing our balance. "You took gymnastics last year!"

"And how about when you told him you couldn't get over the wall unless he let you stand on his shoulders?" Lauren raised her eyebrows at Stephanie. "If we could make it over, you could."

"I didn't feel very confident just then," Stephanie said nonchalantly.

"Yeah, right. You only acted that way to make him like you," Lauren said. "Just like when you asked that guy to carry your suitcase upstairs. It's all because of that stupid article in *Teen Topics*," she concluded knowingly. "The one that said the best way to interest a boy is to act like you need his help."

"No, it isn't!" Stephanie protested. "Anyway, you're just jealous because he's the cutest guy on this whole campus."

Kate burst out laughing. "Jealous? Ha! Any guy who falls for an act like that is a loser!"

Stephanie smiled. "He's not a loser, and you know it. So quit being so jealous. It's not *my* fault he likes me."

"Yeah, well, just wait until he finds out who the real you is," Kate said. "Once you start telling him what to do all the time, see how much he likes you."

Stephanie glared at Kate. "Are you saying I'm bossy?"

"Takes one to know one," Lauren whispered to

63

me, and I started laughing. It felt great to let loose and really laugh — I hadn't relaxed once since we'd gotten there.

"Be careful, Patti, you wouldn't want to choke," Jenny suddenly said. "I mean, on top of everything else."

I looked up and saw her and Angela standing there, holding their trays.

"Sorry, there's no room at our table," Lauren said quickly.

"Ginger saved us seats," Angela told her smugly.

"How thrilling for you," Kate muttered.

I waited for them to move on, but they didn't budge.

"Patti, how's your head?" Jenny asked.

"It's fine," I said through clenched teeth.

"Really? I thought you might have a headache," Jenny said. "I mean, you did hit the floor pretty hard." She smiled at me.

I felt like punching her in the nose, which is pretty unusual for me. "Why don't you — " I began.

"Patti's fine, but now that *you're* here she *is* getting a headache," Lauren interrupted me.

All of a sudden I didn't know who was making me angrier — Jenny or Lauren! Jenny was being a

64

creep, as usual, but now Lauren was talking for me —
as if I couldn't take care of myself. Why couldn't
everyone just leave me alone?

"Excuse me," I said, getting up from the table.
"I don't feel very well."

"She's probably still a little woozy," I heard
Jenny say as I walked away. I thought I heard Kate
say something back, but I didn't catch it.

I walked out of the cafeteria, across the campus,
and down Main Street. There were some cute shops
and a park. It was still light out — the clock on the
bank said it was ten after six. I wondered if my parents
and my brother were eating dinner. We usually eat
at around six.

To tell you the truth, I couldn't wait to get home.
I'd never felt so homesick in my life, and I'd only
been gone for twenty-four hours! If I could have gone
home that minute, I probably would have.

If people weren't making fun of me, they were
trying to take care of me. Lauren was acting super-
nice to me, but I didn't know what to say to her. I
hadn't seen Henry since right after I had fainted, and
I didn't want to. Jenny and Ginger were going to
make the rest of the trip miserable for me — so why
should I stay?

Then again, I didn't really want to run away. My

friends would probably worry about me, and people would talk about what a wimp I was. All day long, the workshop directors had been encouraging us to act boldly. Kate was always telling me I needed to have more confidence in myself. That was the problem, actually. Kate, Stephanie, and Lauren had all been telling me what to do, all the time. Stephanie picked out my clothes, Kate told me what to say, and Lauren — well, she had gone even farther than that.

I had to get everyone off my back, and start acting more boldly, on my own. Running away certainly wasn't the answer. I headed slowly back to campus.

"Patti, where did you go?" Lauren asked when I met everyone in the main dorm lounge later that evening.

"I just went for a walk," I explained. "I needed some air."

"Jenny's such a pill," Stephanie commented.

"Tell me something I don't know," Kate said. She patted the couch. "Sit down next to me, Patti."

I sat down and looked around. I spotted Jenny sitting across the room next to Ginger, Christy, and Angela. I guess the two terrible twosomes had become a horrible foursome! Almost all the girls from our dorm were in the lounge, and so were the boys from the dorm next door. "Did you start doing anything yet?" I asked.

Stephanie shook her head. "Nope. They said we're going to play some games."

"I know — Follow the *Leader*!" Lauren cried. Some of the girls from our floor laughed.

"I think the counselors are going to perform a skit," Kate told me. "And we're going to play charades later and do some other stuff."

"Where's the live band?" one boy called out.

"Yeah, I thought we were supposed to have a party," another boy added.

"It's tomorrow night," Stephanie told them, smiling.

"Gee, I hope it's as much fun as this," the first one said, making a face.

Stephanie giggled. "I know, this is kind of lame."

"Here she goes again," Kate whispered to me.

I bit my lip to keep from laughing as our dorm counselors jumped up on the makeshift stage in the middle of the lounge.

"If you thought you were all done for the day, think again!" our floor counselor, MaryAnn, said cheerfully. "Tonight we'll work on your interpersonal skills."

"Our inter *what?*" I heard a familiar voice shout from behind me. I turned around and saw Henry. He smiled at me.

"Your people skills," MaryAnn said. "It's important to relate to other people if you want to be an effective leader."

"So, let's begin!" Tom, the other counselor, cried. "Heads up!" Suddenly, he started tossing oranges into the air. Kids scrambled all around the room trying to catch them. I didn't get one, but out of the corner of my eye I saw Henry catch one.

"Now, pick a person holding an orange and stand near them," Tom instructed us. "There should be no more than ten people in each group."

I didn't see anyone else I knew holding an orange, so I ran over to Henry. "Hi," I said nervously.

"Hey," he said with a grin.

He was still talking to me! I looked around the lounge. Lauren and Kate were standing with the other girls from our floor. Across the room, Stephanie was gazing up at Mr. Wonderful — Chip — and smiling. He was holding an orange.

"So what are we doing, making orange juice for

68

breakfast tomorrow?'' Henry asked me.

I laughed. "It'd probably taste better than the cafeteria's."

"Okay!" MaryAnn shouted. "Each group, get in line, single file. The person holding the orange should put it under his or her neck. Then pass it to the person behind you, all the way down the line, and back. The group that finishes first, wins!"

"What do we win?" one kid called out.

Good question, I thought to myself. It was important to know these things *before* you got involved.

"We have grab bags of snacks and toys up here for the lucky winners," Tom said. "Not that luck is involved — it's teamwork, all the way. Ready?"

Henry tucked the orange under his chin. "I feel like an idiot," he managed to say.

"I know what you mean," I said, laughing.

"On your mark, get set, GO!" Tom yelled.

I looked at Henry. Were we really supposed to pass the orange with our necks?

"Come on, hurry up!" the girl in back of me yelled.

I took a deep breath and moved closer to Henry. I felt stupid, but I figured Henry did, too, so it wasn't that bad. It sure felt funny to be so close to him, though. I maneuvered the orange onto my neck as quickly as I could, and then passed it to the girl behind me.

"Is this what world leaders do at those summit things?" Henry asked me.

"I don't think so," I said. Good old Henry — he always cheered me up. He could make the most embarrassing thing funny.

Somewhere across the room Ginger was yelling, "Come on, Christy — no, not like that!" I turned and saw her picking up their orange from the floor.

"Come on!" the girl behind me yelled. I jerked around. The orange was already back to her, so I grabbed it with my chin and passed it to Henry.

"Done!" he cried, holding the orange up in the air. But we were too late — another group had already finished.

We didn't win any of the other races that night, either, but I didn't care. It was fun just being in Henry's group.

I guess it was a good thing I had stuck around!

Chapter
8

"It looked like you were kissing Henry!" Stephanie said.

"I was not," I said, blushing.

"I got stuck next to the world's most uncoordinated person," Kate grumbled. "We came in last every time, I think."

Lauren opened the door to our suite and we walked in. "At least Ginger and Christy's team didn't win," she said, sinking into a chair in the common room. "There's some justice in the world."

"I think Christy dropped the orange so many times they ended up eating it instead of passing it," Stephanie said. She sat on the windowsill and looked outside.

"You're not watching for that Chip person, are

you?" asked Kate, sitting down on the couch. I took a seat on the couch next to Kate.

Stephanie sighed. "He is *so* cute."

"Too bad you didn't get to stand next to him tonight," said Lauren. "You two might be married by now."

"I think he's kind of shy," Stephanie said. "I like that. I'm going to ask him for his address tomorrow. Northfield's not that far away. Maybe he could visit sometime."

"Yeah, in six years when he gets his driver's license," Kate said skeptically.

"He's twelve," Stephanie said. "Only four years."

"Whatever," Kate said.

"I can see it now." Lauren crossed her legs and leaned back in her chair. "Girl meets boy at conference. They fall in love. They write each other every night, but their parents won't let them call because it's long distance . . . kind of like *Romeo and Juliet*. Then one day, about a week later, the girl forgets all about him because she sees this boy at school . . . let's call him Taylor Sprouts."

"Stop!" Stephanie cried. Kate and I were laughing hysterically. "This is serious," Stephanie said.

"Mm-hm," Kate said, nodding, "I bet it is."

We all started laughing even harder.

The door to our suite opened and our roommates for the weekend strolled into the room. "Oh, *you're* here," Ginger said, frowning.

"Yes, we happen to live here," Stephanie replied.

"*We* want to use the common room," Jenny declared.

"That's nice," Lauren said. "Maybe later."

Ginger put her hands on her hips and glared at us for a minute. When we didn't move, she gave an exasperated sigh. "Come on," she said to her roommates, "we don't want to hang out with them anyway."

"You're right about that!" Jenny added. They walked into their room. I thought they were going to slam the door, but they left it open.

"Since when does Jenny follow Ginger's orders?" Stephanie asked in a soft voice.

I shrugged.

"They're acting like they're best friends all of a sudden," Lauren commented. "Well, they *do* have a lot in common. Nastiness, rudeness — "

She was interrupted by a loud screech from the other room. Then Ginger stormed out into the common room. "All right, who did this?" she asked, pointing to her shirt. There was a big blue stain on it.

"I don't know what you're talking about," Kate said. "We're sitting in here — how could we have done anything?"

"You left this pen on my desk," said Ginger. "When I picked it up to see what it was, it squirted ink all over me!" Jenny, Angela, and Christy came out of the room and stood behind her.

"We didn't even go in your room," said Lauren.

"Oh, yeah? Well, explain this!" Ginger pointed to her shirt again.

"I don't see anything," I said meekly. It was true. The ink stain had completely vanished!

"Look at this! It's horrible." Ginger glanced down at her shirt, and then looked up with startled eyes. Then she examined her shirt again. "Wait a second. What happened?"

"Maybe you should get your eyes checked," Stephanie said with a giggle.

"Now I *know* one of you did it," Ginger said. "And it had to be Kate."

"Me? I didn't do anything!" Kate protested. But she didn't sound very sorry — or very innocent, either. She and Ginger had never gotten along. They had clashed the first time they met, and it had been all downhill from there.

"Maybe you should get the pen checked for fingerprints," Christy suggested.

"This isn't TV," Ginger grumbled. Sometimes it seemed like Christy's elevator didn't go all the way to the top. "Just make sure you stay out of our room from now on," Ginger said, glaring at Kate.

"Okay, fine," Kate said. She stood up and brushed off her jeans. "Come on, let's go into our room. If we stay out here they might arrest us." Lauren, Stephanie, and I laughed and followed her into the bedroom.

"Is anyone else besides me starving?" Lauren asked. "I think I have a few cookies left." She reached under the bed to get her tin. "Now where did I leave — whoa!" she suddenly screamed, yanking her arm out from underneath the bed.

"What is it?" asked Kate, laughing. "Can't you find your cookies?"

"Ha-ha. Very funny." Lauren frowned at her. "It just so happens that there's a mouse under my bed."

"Gross!" Stephanie rushed to her bed and sat down, pulling her legs up underneath her.

"Are you serious?" I asked. "There's a mouse in here?"

"I'm not surprised, considering how old this dorm is," Kate said calmly.

"Yeah, but we're on the third floor. Aren't they supposed to stay in the basement or something?" Lauren asked, looking warily under the bed.

"Who cares?" Stephanie demanded. "The question is, what are we going to *do* about it? I am not spending the night in the same room as a mouse!"

"Yeah, there's barely enough room for four *people* in here," I said, laughing.

Stephanie just stared at me as if I were crazy. Mice didn't bother me, though. I don't love them, but I'm not afraid of them. My little brother Horace has a few mice for pets.

"I guess we could get our dorm counselor," suggested Kate.

"Let's make Jenny get rid of it," said Lauren. "Better yet, if we capture it, maybe we can put it in their room!"

"I don't care where it goes — just get it out of here!" Stephanie cried.

Kate was leaning way over in her chair, staring under Lauren's bed. "Either that mouse is really nervous, or else it's dead," she said. "It hasn't moved in about a minute."

"Yuck — a dead mouse!" Stephanie stuck out her tongue. "Just think, it was in here last night, too."

"Too bad Chip isn't here. He could protect you," Lauren teased her.

"I don't see you doing anything," Stephanie shot back.

"Don't worry, I'll take care of it," I said. I got up and walked over to Lauren's bed. Then I got down on my hands and knees.

"Be careful, Patti — it might bite you," Stephanie warned.

"No, it won't," I told her. I looked at the mouse for a minute. It most definitely was not moving. It wasn't alive, either. I reached in, grabbed it, and held it up in front of everyone. "It's fake!" I told them, smiling.

"You're not kidding, are you?" Lauren asked.

"No, look. It's made out of plastic, and then this phony fur is glued on." I passed it around to everybody.

Stephanie didn't want to touch it. "It looks real enough to me," she muttered.

"What would a fake mouse be doing underneath

77

your bed?" Kate wondered out loud.

"Obviously someone wanted to play a practical joke," Lauren said. "And I have a good idea who!" She got up and charged into the common room. We followed her.

"What was all that yelling about?" Jenny asked, lounging on the couch. "Did you look in the mirror?" Angela giggled.

Lauren held the mouse up by its tail. "Look what I found under my bed."

"Eww!" all four of them yelled at once.

"Quit pretending," Lauren said, swinging the mouse around in the air. "You know this is a fake."

"No, I didn't," Ginger said, moving away as Lauren swung the mouse in front of her. "Honest."

"Well, how did it get under my bed?" Lauren asked.

"I don't know. How did that pen get on my desk?" Ginger argued loudly.

There was a knock on the door, and our floor counselor, MaryAnn, poked her head into the room. "Is everything all right in here?"

Lauren hid the mouse behind her back, and no one said anything for a second.

"Yes, everything's fine," Kate finally said.

78

"I thought I heard you screaming," MaryAnn said, looking curious.

"Oh — we were just laughing," Ginger explained in a sweet voice. None of us wanted to get in trouble!

"Well, try to keep the noise down," MaryAnn said. "Some kids might be trying to sleep, okay?"

"Okay," Stephanie answered.

MaryAnn smiled and shut the door.

"So, do you want to explain how that pen got into my room?" Ginger demanded as soon as MaryAnn was gone.

"Maybe someone in the dorm is playing practical jokes," Stephanie suggested.

"And maybe someone in this *room* is," Kate said, glaring at Jenny.

"It could be anyone," I said. "We don't lock our door, remember?"

"Well, maybe we should start," Ginger said. "Come on, let's go hide all our stuff," she instructed her roommates. They stood up, walked back into their room, and shut the door.

Lauren tossed the plastic mouse into the trash can and brushed off her hands. "Maybe now we can have some cookies," she said.

"Better make sure they're not phony, too," Kate advised.

We went back to our room, ate the cookies, and talked for a while. Stephanie read her horoscope in *Star Turns* and decided Chip must be a Leo, or else they wouldn't be hitting it off so well. Then she and Kate got into a big argument about whether or not to believe in astrology. Kate doesn't believe in any of that stuff; she calls it "mumbo jumbo." Stephanie and Lauren think it makes a lot of sense. I don't know. Sometimes the predictions come true, and sometimes they don't. I wouldn't exactly organize my life around them — but sometimes Stephanie does.

Around midnight we were all so sleepy we yawned every time we opened our mouths to say something, so we decided to go to bed. The other bedroom was pretty quiet. It sounded as if they were getting ready for bed, too.

Kate and I were in the bathroom brushing our teeth when we heard Jenny shriek. Not again!

Kate wiped her mouth with a towel. "She has the most obnoxious laugh I've ever heard," she said.

Suddenly the bathroom door banged open and Jenny almost flew in, with Angela right behind her as usual. Jenny's face was pale white, and she was holding a big black spider as far away from her as she could. She put it down on the sink.

Kate jumped back. "What are you doing?"

"Just returning something of yours," Jenny said angrily. "I found it under my pillow where you left it!"

Kate stared at the spider. "It — it is a fake, isn't it?"

"Stop fooling around. It isn't funny," Jenny said. "I don't want you to go into our room ever again!"

"I didn't!" Kate said. "I haven't been in there once. I was downstairs all night — you saw me."

"Well, I don't know how you did it, but I know you did it," Jenny said. "Just keep out of our stuff from now on, or you'll be sorry," she warned.

"I didn't do anything!" Kate wailed as Jenny and Angela stormed out of the bathroom.

"I know that," I said sympathetically, "but they don't."

"Who do you think is doing all this?" Kate asked me.

"I'm not sure, but I think it's probably some of the boys," I said, running the hot water so I could wash my face. "All that stuff could have been in the grab bags the kids won downstairs tonight."

Kate's eyes lit up. "That's it! Maybe we can catch them in the act tomorrow," she said, brushing her hair. "Then the roommates from another planet will stop accusing *me*." She picked the fat, rubbery spider out of the sink and rubbed it between her palms. "You know what, Patti?" She laughed. "I almost wish I *had* put this under Jenny's pillow. What a great idea!"

Chapter
9

When I woke up the next morning, I felt a hundred percent better than the day before. I didn't have to give a speech, and I'd had a lot of fun hanging out with Henry and my friends the night before.

I got up a little earlier than everyone else so I could have first dibs on the shower. I was sick of fighting our roommates for the bathroom, and I wanted to make sure I got hot water this time! No one else was up, and the quiet was a nice change.

I combed my wet hair in the bathroom, brushed my teeth, and did a few other little things — like put on lotion — before I went back to our room. When I was leaving, Angela stumbled out of her bedroom with a towel over her shoulder, rubbing her eyes. She went into the bathroom without saying good morning and turned on the shower. I went back to the room.

Kate and Stephanie were awake by then, and were trying to get Lauren out of bed. Lauren is late for everything if you don't watch her. She'd *almost* rather stay in bed than eat breakfast!

Kate shook her arm. "Come on, Lauren, they might have pancakes," she said.

Lauren's eyes popped open. "I'm up," she said.

I was trying to figure out what to wear when there was a loud knock on the door. "Uh-oh," Kate said. "It's the roommate police again."

Since I was the closest, I opened it. Angela was standing in the doorway, her mousy brown hair dripping water all over the floor. She had a white towel wrapped around her — only it looked like it was covered with dirt. She glared at us angrily.

"What's wrong?" I asked. "Isn't there any hot water left?"

Angela held out a bar of soap. "I'm going to kill whoever put this in the shower," she said through clenched teeth.

"What's the matter, don't you use soap?" Stephanie joked.

Angela scowled at her. "As if you don't know!"

"Yeah, soap happens to work well on dirt," Kate observed, staring at Angela's filthy towel.

"I'm dirtier now than I was when I went into the shower!" Angela exclaimed. "Thanks to this dumb soap you left there, Lauren."

"Me?" Lauren cried, sitting up in bed.

"Yeah, I saw you leaving the bathroom this morning," Angela said. "You put the soap in the shower for me." She rubbed it against her arm. "It makes *black* lather!"

"I haven't even gotten out of bed yet!" Lauren protested.

Angela didn't even notice that I was the one with wet hair, wearing a robe.

"Sure you didn't! I'm going back to the shower," Angela said, "and wash this junk off me!" She slammed the bar of soap down on my dresser and sashayed back into the bathroom.

After she left, I shut the door and the four of us cracked up laughing.

"You're lucky you picked the other shower," Kate told me.

"I know!" I said. "That soap looks horrible."

"I wonder who put that soap in their shower," Lauren said.

"I don't know who's doing all this, but they're

pretty good, whoever they are," Stephanie said, shaking her head.

"You know what? It's probably someone like Henry," I said. I hated to blame him, but it did make sense.

"Boys aren't allowed in the dorm, remember?" Kate said.

"Well, if it wasn't him, and it wasn't us, who was it?" Lauren asked.

I shrugged. "Beats me!"

After breakfast, we had to go to the auditorium for a lecture. We found four seats together at the end of a row. A group of teachers sat down across the aisle from us.

"So much for sneaking out," Lauren mumbled.

It felt strange to be back in the auditorium. Just looking at the stage made my knees feel wobbly. I took a deep breath. *That's all over now,* I reminded myself.

"Good morning!" Ms. Hayes said into the microphone just as the clock on the wall struck nine o'clock. "We are very fortunate to have our next guest with us. He's one of the country's experts on what makes today's political, social, and spiritual leaders what they are — leaders. Will you please

welcome Dr. Jerome Cathcart!'' Ms. Hayes smiled
and stepped back from the podium.

We all applauded. Dr. Cathcart walked up to
the microphone. It looked as if he were carrying an
entire novel. He put a huge stack of papers on the
podium, adjusted his reading glasses, and began
speaking. ''We are gathered here together — ''

''What is he doing, performing a marriage ceremony?'' Lauren whispered.

''To study the impact of leaders on our society,''
Dr. Cathcart went on. ''And to learn what we can
about our own potential for leadership. Since you
children are the leaders of tomorrow, I think it is
important to study which leaders in the past have
succeeded, and which have failed, and why. . . .''

''Oh, ugh,'' a kid behind me groaned.

Dr. Cathcart must have talked for about half an
hour without saying anything interesting. It was torture! He didn't have any interesting stories or slides.
He just kept droning on, stopping now and then to
shuffle his papers.

I think Kate was the only one in the whole auditorium who was listening. Stephanie was looking
all over the place, trying to find out where Chip was
sitting. I was afraid she was going to strain her neck!
Lauren was sitting next to me, on the aisle. Her eyes

87

had been closed for the last ten minutes. Her left elbow was on the armrest, and she was holding her head up with her hand.

I wondered if I should wake her up before one of the teachers noticed. They seemed to be totally absorbed in the speech, though, so I decided not to bother.

About five minutes later, Lauren let out a tiny snore — then her arm slipped off the armrest, and she jerked her head up with a start.

I heard the kids behind us start to snicker. Across the aisle, one of the chaperons was staring at Lauren with a disapproving look on her face. She was sitting on the end, so she got up and crept over to Lauren.

"Please try to show some respect, young lady," the teacher said softly. "Dr. Cathcart is a very important man, and you can learn a lot from him. If you need a nap, take it during lunch!"

Almost the whole row in front of us turned around and stared at Lauren.

"Yes, I will, thank you," Lauren said, blushing.

"Now, pay attention!" the teacher ordered Lauren. "I'll be watching you." Then she returned to her seat.

Lauren nodded and turned to face the stage. She rubbed her eyes and tried to focus on Dr. Cathcart.

Kate nudged me with her elbow. "What happened?" she whispered.

"Lauren fell asleep," I said quietly.

"And next time, try not to snore!" a boy behind us said loudly, so that everyone in the area could hear him.

I felt bad for Lauren, but it was nice to see *her* face turn red for once!

Half an hour later Dr. Cathcart was *still* talking. It was ten o'clock and he hadn't even made it to the twentieth century! I heard a ripping noise and looked over to see Stephanie tearing off a piece of her program. She took the cap off her pen and started writing something.

"What's she doing?" I whispered to Kate.

"It's a note to Chip," Kate answered softly. "He's about four rows away." She turned to Stephanie. "Everyone in here is going to see your note if you try to pass it."

"But I want to make sure I get his address," she complained. "What if I don't find him again?"

Kate shrugged. "You'll live."

I held my finger to my lips to tell them to be quiet. The teacher who was watching Lauren like a hawk had her eye on the rest of us, too. I didn't want to get in trouble.

Dr. Cathcart paused to rearrange his papers. He took a sip of water, and I thought maybe he had finished without anyone noticing. No such luck. He plunged back into his speech.

Stephanie was tapping both of her feet on the floor. She looked like she was going to die of impatience. Finally, she decided to send her note. I watched her write: *I'm four rows behind you, three seats over. Turn around! — S.*

She tapped the girl in front of her and whispered where to pass the note. I held my breath and watched the note make its way to Chip. Everyone turned around to see who had sent it, and some kids waved or made funny faces.

When the note got to Chip, he turned around, looking confused.

"You should have put your name on it," Kate whispered.

"He knows it's me," Stephanie said confidently. She grinned at Chip. "Hi," she mouthed to him.

He smiled and was about to turn back around when Stephanie whispered loudly, "Wait!" She held up her program and pretended to write something on it. "Send me your address," she mouthed.

Chip didn't seem to understand what she was saying.

"Write down your address," she mouthed, gesturing toward the piece of paper with her pen.

"What?" Chip whispered.

"He may be cute, but he's a little on the dumb side," Kate said dryly.

Stephanie hurried to scribble another note on her program. This time she wrote in big letters, *GIVE ME YOUR ADDRESS!* She held it up so Chip could see it.

There were too many heads in the way — he was straining to read it. He shook his head and mouthed, "I don't get it."

Stephanie sighed with exasperation. "I said, give me your address!" This time her voice came out, loud and clear, for *everyone* to hear.

Kids all around us burst out laughing. Half were staring at Chip, and half were pointing at Stephanie and chuckling. Even Dr. Cathcart stopped talking to see what the commotion was all about.

Chip turned around as fast as he could, and Stephanie slouched down in her seat.

"Nice going," Kate whispered, giggling.

"Is everything all right out there?" Dr. Cathcart asked, peering at the crowd over his reading glasses.

Stephanie folded her arms across her chest. Her face was bright pink — even her *ears* were blushing!

The only person staring straight ahead was Lauren. The teacher who had spoken to her was still watching her every move.

Maybe it's a boring lecture, but the morning has been anything but boring! I thought as I relaxed in my seat. I was glad I wasn't the *only* one who could embarrass herself in front of hundreds! You know what they say, humiliation loves company . . . or something like that.

"So which one of you wants to wear this?" Kate held up a large paper bag. "Lauren the Snorer, or Stephanie the Boy Chaser?"

"Maybe you could just bring us our lunch?" Lauren asked, sliding onto the couch in our common room.

Stephanie sank into a chair. "I'm never leaving this suite again," she said.

"I thought you guys told me yesterday it was no big deal," I reminded them. "Remember? You said everyone would forget all about it."

"Well . . . yeah," Lauren said. "But all you did was faint. I snored!"

But that was your fault, not mine, I thought, *and that's the big difference.* I didn't say anything, though. I was still upset with Lauren for what she had done to me, but I didn't want to have a fight about it.

"You could always go one at a time," Kate said. She held the paper bag up to Stephanie. "I don't know if this is going to fit over all that hair, though."

"Oh, very funny." Stephanie punched a hole in the bag.

"Just wait until *you* do something stupid," Lauren said. "Then you'll be sorry you treated us this way."

"It'll never happen," Kate said breezily.

"We'll see about that," Lauren muttered.

I heard some loud voices outside the door. "Brace yourselves," I said. "Here come our roommates."

Stephanie jumped up from her chair. "Quick! Let's go into our — "

"Well, if it isn't Sleepy and Dopey," Ginger said, striding into the common room. Jenny and Angela cackled with laughter.

"So, *did* he give you his address?" Jenny asked.

Stephanie looked as if she were ready to pounce on both of them. "Not yet," she muttered.

"Lauren, you should get more sleep at night," Jenny said. "Then these embarrassing things wouldn't happen to you."

93

Ginger shook her head and laughed. "You know, you guys are giving Riverhurst a bad name. First Patti passes out, then Lauren snores in public — "

"I was *not* snoring," Lauren replied angrily.

"That's not what I heard," Angela said snottily.

"Let's get out of here before anyone finds out we're in the same room with them," Jenny said. She turned on her heel.

"Oh, brother," Kate whispered.

"Wait a sec — I need to get something. And there better not be anything in here," Ginger said to us as she walked toward their bedroom. They had posted another big KEEP OUT! sign on their door. "I'm sick of those stupid practical jokes."

"So am I," Jenny said. "I mean, how immature!" She turned the knob on their door.

"Let's go to the cafeteria," Stephanie said. "Anywhere is better than here!"

We stood up and walked to the door. We were halfway out when we heard four shrieks — and a loud splash! It sounded like someone had turned on the shower!

I turned around. Ginger and Jenny were standing in their doorway, dripping with water! Christy and Angela had been following them, as usual, so they weren't *quite* as wet, but they looked just as angry. Christy's hair was plastered to her head on one side.

"Wh — what happened?" Lauren gasped, laughing.

"Did you guys need another shower?" Stephanie asked.

Ginger pointed to the top of the door. A plastic bucket was perched there, attached to some rope. "You rigged this up!"

Christy jumped up and grabbed the bucket. "I told you we should have checked for fingerprints."

"You're not going to get away with this!" Ginger cried, squeezing the bottom of her soaked sweatshirt.

"We didn't do it!" Kate yelled.

"Yeah, sure!" Jenny replied, peeling her shirt-sleeve off her arm. "We'll get you back, just watch!"

"We didn't do anything!" Lauren protested. "It must have been one of your secret admirers."

Christy had run into the bathroom, and she came back carrying the bucket — full of water. "Get them!" Ginger screamed.

We flew out the door and raced down the hall. I could hear Christy running behind us, and the water sloshing out of the bucket onto the carpet.

"Hold it!" a voice cried. We turned and saw MaryAnn standing in front of Christy. "What's going on? Where do you think you're going with that bucket?"

We left Christy to explain and escaped down the stairs, taking them two at a time. "That was close!" Stephanie said when we got outside.

"Too close," Lauren said, panting. "Considering we didn't do anything. At least I didn't. Did you?" she asked Kate.

"Me? No! What about you?" Kate asked Stephanie.

She shook her head. "I didn't touch their stuff."

"Well, I hope whoever it is leaves them alone from now on," Kate said as we walked across campus to the dining hall. "Otherwise we'll be in big trouble."

"I think we already are," I said.

On our way to the cafeteria we passed a group of boys playing catch on the lawn. I thought I recognized them from the auditorium.

"Hey, wake up!" one of them yelled at Lauren.

"Yeah, aren't you supposed to be taking your nap now?" another added. They all started laughing loudly.

"Oh, shut up," Lauren mumbled.

Chapter 10

"I hope this workshop is better than that lecture was this morning," Henry grumbled.

"So do I," I said. "I don't think I could take much more of that." We were in a large classroom, waiting for the rest of the kids to arrive.

Ginger, Jenny, Christy, and Angela were huddled together on the other side of the room. That wasn't anything new, really, but I had a funny feeling they were up to something — like planning their revenge on us. I was worried. It was bad enough to have Jenny and Angela against us, or Ginger and Christy as enemies. But the four of them working together — that meant they'd give us twice as much trouble, at least. Jenny and Ginger were a lethal combination.

Mrs. Mead and one of the workshop counselors came into the room and shut the door. It was nice to see Mrs. Mead — we hadn't been in one of her groups yet.

"Please, take your seats," Mrs. Mead said. "This is Joanne Mitchell, and she'll be helping us with today's workshop."

I sat down next to Henry. The chair on the other side of me was empty, but just then the door opened and Lauren walked into the room. "Sorry," she said to Mrs. Mead. "I got lost." She scooted into the other seat next to me.

"The title of today's workshop is 'Assertiveness Training,' " Mrs. Mead continued. "Being assertive means standing up for yourself. But, there's a difference between being assertive and being *aggressive*, as we'll learn this afternoon. Joanne, why don't you take over?"

Joanne smiled at all of us. "Choosing something you would like to do and following through on it is being assertive," she said. "Like coming to this conference. Or entering your essay in the contest." Joanne looked at me and smiled.

I'm not the assertive one, I wanted to say.

The more Joanne talked about what it meant to stand up for yourself, the more I realized I hardly

98

ever did. When we went to the movies, if I got the worst seat, I didn't say anything. If we went out to eat and the waiter brought me something I didn't order, I ate it anyway. I thought it was just part of being nice. And being nice is important to me.

That weekend there had been lots of times I could have been more assertive. Like when we chose our beds in our room — I didn't even get to choose mine. I settled for last choice. I didn't know how much I could do about it, though. When your best friends are people like Kate and Stephanie, even if you are assertive, they're *more* assertive.

I couldn't believe how upset I was getting, sitting there. Friends aren't supposed to feel that way about each other. Then I remembered all the times Stephanie and Kate had gotten into fights, and all the arguments Lauren and Kate had. They had always made up. Maybe it was okay to feel angry toward a friend sometimes.

"What I'd like you to do is to turn to the person on your right, starting with you." Joanne pointed to the person on the end of our large semicircle. "That person will be your partner."

Heads kept turning as we went around the circle. I was kind of worried. If Henry was my partner, and I was supposed to practice being assertive, did that mean I had to tell him I liked him? Or ask him on a date or something?

Then again, I didn't know if I wanted to be paired with Lauren, either. I wasn't sure I'd be able to tell her how I really felt.

The person in front of Henry turned to him, so they were partners. I turned my head a little and looked at Lauren. "I guess we're partners," I said, trying to smile.

"Good," Lauren said.

Stephanie was paired with a girl from another town, and Kate was stuck with Karla Stamos. I felt sorry for Karla. No question about who was more assertive there!

"The first thing I'd like you to do is to spend a few minutes getting to know each other," Joanne said. "But if you already do, you can go right ahead to the exercises."

Henry raised his hand. "Are we doing sit-ups, or push-ups?" he asked.

"Neither," Joannne replied, smiling politely at Henry's joke. "We're going to practice something called 'honest feedback.' " She handed a pile of papers to the girl at the beginning of the semicircle and asked her to pass them around. "This sheet will explain everything," she said. "But if you have any questions, you can ask me or Mrs. Mead. We'll be walking around to see how you're getting along."

I took a sheet and handed the rest to Lauren. I skimmed it quickly. It didn't look too bad — then I got to question number three: "Suppose your partner has just gone behind your back and done something you didn't like — without telling you. How would you respond? Remember — be honest!"

Maybe we won't have time for that one, I thought, glancing at my watch. But the workshop was scheduled to last another hour.

"Okay, people, get started. And remember, you can be assertive and still be nice!" Joanne instructed us. *Really?* I thought.

The first two questions weren't too hard. Lauren and I had to tell each other what we liked and disliked about the conference, to practice expressing our opinion to other people.

"I like that there are so many people here," Lauren said. "And I like living in a dorm with you, Kate, and Stephanie. I don't like the food, and I definitely don't like our other roommates. Now you go," she told me.

"Okay . . . I, uh, like the dorm. And I've met

some nice people on our floor," I said. "That's it."

"You forgot to say your dislikes," Lauren reminded me.

"Oh, right." I paused. How was I going to put this? "I don't like some of the activities," I began. "Like that lecture this morning. And," I said, trying to stay calm, "I didn't like when I had to — "

"How are you two doing?" Joanne interrupted, smiling at us.

"No problem," Lauren said. "We're always honest with each other."

Well, not always, I thought.

"Keep up the good work," Joanne told us, and moved on.

"What were you saying?" Lauren asked.

"Oh. Never mind," I said, shrugging. "I can't remember anyway." *Come on, Patti, be assertive,* one voice in my head said. But the other said, *Don't bring it up and get into a fight in front of everybody.*

The next question was really boring. It said, "Describe your partner's appearance." It only took a second to do that.

"Okay, on to number three." Lauren picked up her sheet.

I felt the bongo drums start beating in my stomach again. "You go first," I told Lauren.

"Okay." Lauren tapped her pencil against the desk. "This is hard. I can't imagine you ever doing anything I didn't like, or going behind my back!" She paused. "But if you did, I guess I'd tell you never to do it again. Right?" She smiled at me.

"I wouldn't ever go behind your back," I said. *Come on, Patti,* that assertive voice inside my head said again. I took a deep breath. "But you did that to me," I said softly.

Lauren looked shocked. "What?"

"When I read this question, I thought, I don't have to pretend, because this just happened to me." My hands were shaking. It was so hard to tell her how I felt! "When you sent in my paper, you went behind my back. And then when I got here and I found out I had to give a speech, I thought I was going to die. You *know* how much I hate getting up in front of people. But you did it anyway," I said.

"I — I didn't know you were going to have to do that," she answered.

"You should have found out first," I told her. "I would have. I'd never make you do something you didn't want to do."

"But, Patti, I thought you would win something really great," Lauren said. "Your essay was so good, you deserved to win! And I thought since you were too timid to enter the contest, I'd do it for you."

"Well, you shouldn't have," I said firmly. "It's up to me to decide stuff like that. Lauren, I fainted in front of *everybody*. I felt like such an idiot. I wanted to go home!"

Lauren's eyes were all watery and she looked like she was about to start crying. "I'm sorry," she said. "I'm really, really sorry."

"It never would have happened if you hadn't decided something for me," I said. "That's the main point. You can't run my life."

"I never meant to," Lauren said softly. "Honest, Patti. I would never try to hurt you."

"I know," I said, nodding. "But you did." I didn't know what else to say after that. Were we still friends? I felt both relieved and terrible at the same time.

"Patti, I only did it because I like you so much. I wanted other people to see how talented you are," Lauren said, wiping a tear away with her hand. "I'm sorry!"

Just looking at her made me start crying, too. "It's okay," I told her, my voice trembling. "I guess it's not really your fault I fainted."

"I told you to eat breakfast," Lauren said, smiling as she brushed another tear away.

"Yeah, well, at least I didn't snore!" I said, sniffling a little. It felt great to get all the tension out in the open. I didn't feel angry anymore!

"Seriously, though, I promise not to make your decisions for you," Lauren said. "I know you know what you're doing, and you don't need my help."

"I didn't say *that*," I said. "Just don't do anything without telling me about it, okay?"

"Okay." Lauren held out her hand to shake mine, and I reached over and hugged her. Luckily, everyone was so busy doing their exercises that no one noticed us crying or hugging.

"Okay, next exercise!" Lauren said, trying to smile. "Make a list of your fears, and discuss ways of overcoming them. Patti, you go first. I mean — if you want to. If you don't, then I can go. Whatever — you decide," she said.

I laughed. "I'll start. This is easy. My number-one fear is getting up in front of a huge crowd of people!"

"Let's see . . . how could you get over that?" Lauren asked in a serious voice. "Let me think. I know! You could borrow that paper bag of Kate's and cut eyeholes in it so you could read your speech!"

I cracked up at the image of me on stage wearing a paper bag, and so did Lauren.

Joanne came over and stood next to us. "Girls, are you working on an exercise?" she asked.

Lauren nodded. "We're expressing ourselves through laughter," she said, giggling.

"Excellent!" Joanne clapped her hands together. "I have an idea — let's see how you're doing so far," she said. "Why don't some of you stand up and show us what you've learned?" She looked around the classroom.

Nobody moved, at first. Then Kate stood up. "Come on, Karla, get *up*," she said. She tugged at Karla's sleeve.

"Well, I can see *you* don't need any practice being assertive," Joanne said, laughing.

"That's right," Kate said smugly.

"This is an example of being too assertive," Joanne explained, pointing to Kate. "There's a difference between being assertive and being bossy."

A couple of kids in the class snickered, and Kate's face turned bright red.

"Now we're four for four," Lauren whispered to me.

"What do you mean?" I whispered back.

"Each one of us has done something totally

embarrassing," she answered. "They should call this the Humiliation Conference!"

I put my hand over my mouth so Joanne wouldn't hear me laughing. It was pretty funny, when you thought about it. We had been so sure we were going to get to know a lot of people. It was true, we had. But everyone knew us for the wrong reasons!

Lauren, we'd better find our own paper bags, I wrote on the exercise sheet. *Kate needs hers!*

Chapter
11

That night there was a dance to celebrate the end of the conference. Actually, they didn't say that was what it was for, but we were all looking forward to going home! Except Stephanie. She wanted to talk to Chip again, so she could get to know him better before we went back to Riverhurst.

The dance was being held in the student union. For the first half hour or so, the girls stayed on one side of the big dance floor, and the boys stayed on the other.

"This is just like home," Stephanie observed, frowning.

"We'd better be careful if we do dance," Kate said. "Ginger might put a banana peel on the floor or something."

Our roommates hadn't done anything to get us yet, but I had a feeling it was only a matter of time. Even though we'd sworn that we hadn't done anything, they were convinced we had.

"Well, I know one thing," Lauren said. "I'm not dancing tonight. I don't want to take any risks."

"Yeah, if we embarrass ourselves again, they probably won't let anyone from Riverhurst come next year," I said.

"Well, I know *I'm* not coming back," Kate said. She was glaring at Joanne, the counselor who had told her she was bossy.

Lauren and I laughed. Stephanie was still scanning the crowd for Chip. "I wish I were taller," she complained. "I can't see him anywhere!"

"Look, some people are actually dancing!" Lauren cried. The deejay was playing pretty good music — like the Boodles, Lavonne, and the Polka Dots.

"There he is!" Stephanie suddenly cried.

"A little louder, please," Kate said. "I don't think everyone in here heard you."

Stephanie ran off to talk to Chip. I spotted them over by the entrance. A few minutes later, one of Stephanie's favorite songs came on, and I saw her dragging him out onto the dance floor.

"Now *that's* too assertive." Kate laughed.

I laughed, too, but I kind of admired Stephanie. I mean, I wanted to ask Henry to dance, but I was too chicken. I thought about all the things we had practiced that afternoon. I could probably ask him to dance without freaking him out. And if he didn't want to, I wouldn't drag him out there.

"Lauren, can I ask you something?" I said. "Would it be totally queer if I asked Henry to dance?"

"I think that's a great idea!" Lauren said, grinning. "But you might not get the chance."

"What do you mean?" I asked her. Then I felt a tap on my shoulder, and turned around. It was Henry!

"Want to do the Honest Feedback Twist?" he asked me.

I could feel my face turning red, but I hoped the room was too dark for him to notice. "Sure," I said. "How does it go?"

"Wait up, you guys!" Stephanie called from the end of the hall. She ran to catch up with us as we started walking up the stairs to our floor.

"So, did you promise to write each other every night forever and ever?" Lauren asked.

"Yeah, you and Chip danced well together," Kate said.

"Oh, please," Stephanie said. "I won't be writing *him* any letters."

"Why not?" I asked.

Stephanie sighed. "He is *such* an airhead. I was telling him about our recycling plan at John's, and he said, 'So do you wash all the cardboard off and use it again?' And he was serious!"

The three of us burst out laughing.

She shook her head. "I don't know what I ever saw in him."

"You said he was the cutest guy on campus, remember?" Kate said as we passed the second floor.

"Well, that's all he has going for him," Stephanie declared. "When they brought out the food, he took off — he didn't even ask me if I wanted any! And he's not such a hot dancer, either. He was just copying all of *my* moves."

"Speaking of dancing, did you catch Henry and Patti out there?" Lauren whistled. "We're talking L-O-V-E."

I hit her on the arm. "We are not!"

"Just do me one favor, Patti," Stephanie said. "When you plan your bridesmaids' dresses, make them red, black, and white!"

We walked down the hall to our room. "Wait a second!" Kate whispered as we opened the door.

111

"They might be trying to ambush us."

We crept through the common room in the darkness, carefully looking in every direction — not that we could see much.

"I think they're still at the dance," Stephanie said. "At least they were there when I left."

"Why didn't you tell me that?" Kate flicked on the light in our room.

I gasped. I couldn't believe what I was seeing! They had said they'd get even with us — but I never dreamed they'd go *this* far!

Yarn was strung all over the room, tied to the bed frames, the lamps, the windows — even our suitcases! Our clothes had been dumped out onto our beds and they were all crumpled up and tied into knots. But the worst thing of all was the floor! It was covered in some kind of green slime, like the kind you can buy at Halloween. The floor looked like a scummy pond!

"That is so gross!" Stephanie said.

"Yuck! They really got us!" Lauren added.

We stood there in shock for a minute or two. "I don't even know if we can walk in there," Kate said. She touched the floor with her sneaker. It made a squishing noise.

Stephanie broke some of the strings of yarn off

the doorway. "This is going to take us all night to clean up," she complained.

"There's shaving cream all over our beds," Lauren pointed out, breaking some yarn so she could get through.

"I'm going to get some scissors from MaryAnn," Kate announced. "I'll see if she has some rags and a bucket, too."

"While you're there, tell her what those jerks did to us!" Stephanie said.

I tried to yank apart the yarn that stood between me and my bed.

"Maybe we should take off our shoes," Lauren said. "That stuff might ruin them."

"I'm not walking in that with bare feet!" Stephanie cried.

Kate came back with the cleaning stuff, and we got to work. First we cut all the yarn apart — it filled the wastebasket! Then we used the rags to scoop up as much of the slime as we could, and dumped it in the bucket. After we rinsed out the bucket in the shower, we filled it with shampoo and water and began washing the floor.

"Why couldn't we stay somewhere with maid service?" Stephanie grumbled when it was her turn to wash.

I untangled all of my clothes, and started packing my duffel bag.

"If I never hear of Montvale College again, I'll be happy!" Lauren said.

"I wonder where the creepheads are," Kate said. "It's after eleven. They'll get in trouble if they stay out late."

"I hope they *do*!" Stephanie said.

Suddenly I heard a loud crash in what sounded like the common room. "Lauren, turn down the radio," I said. "I think I hear something."

When I went out to investigate, I heard someone talking. It sounded like it was coming from the other bedroom. I tiptoed over to it and put my ear against the door.

"I don't know, I think I'd look better with short hair," I heard Jenny saying. "But not *short* short."

"I'm good at cutting hair," Ginger said. "Want me to do it?"

I snickered. That would be the best practical joke of all — Ginger giving Jenny a haircut! I went back to the room to tell everyone our roommates had been there the whole time.

I stopped smiling when I walked in. Everyone was staring at me with weird expressions on their faces. Stephanie had her hands on her hips. Lauren was tapping her foot on a clean part of the floor.

Kate held up a wrinkled paper bag in front of my face.

Uh-oh, I thought.

"Would you like to explain this?" she said, staring at me.

"Is that the bag you told Lauren to wear?" I said, smiling weakly.

Kate reached into the bag and pulled out a pink rubber centipede. Then she took out a can of itching powder and a pack of gum. "We found this under your mattress," she said, "when we were taking the sheets off the beds. Patti, are *you* the one who's been playing all these practical jokes?"

"Me?" I said. "Am *I* the kind of person who'd do something like this?"

"I didn't think so, but yes!" Kate answered. "It was you all along, wasn't it?"

I couldn't keep it a secret any longer. "It was me," I admitted.

Stephanie threw down the sponge. "What! Are you serious?"

"If I wasn't knee-deep in shaving cream, I'd say I admired your work," Lauren grumbled.

"How did you do it?" Kate asked. "Why did you do it?"

"I was tired of them making fun of me. You're always telling me to be bold and stand up for myself. So I did." I shrugged. "I wanted to get them off my back."

"So you put the mouse under my bed, too?" Lauren asked.

"Yeah. I did it to throw them off the track."

"Where'd you get all this stuff?" Kate sniffed the gum. "Is this pepper-flavored?"

"Yeah. I got it at this store nearby, the night I went for a walk. It was pretty easy to set up most of the jokes — those guys were never around," I explained.

"And you put the black soap in the shower that morning when you were in there!" Lauren exclaimed.

"Why didn't you tell us this before?" Stephanie asked. "I would have enjoyed it more, knowing one of *us* was behind it."

"You never asked. You never even thought I was capable of it," I pointed out.

"Well, we never pictured you as the practical joker type," said Kate.

"I know — that's why it was so much fun!" I told them. "I'm sorry about all the mess. I thought they might retaliate, but I didn't know it would be

116

this bad. That's why I didn't use the rest of the stuff I got. After yesterday I could tell they were really mad."

"I hated cleaning up, but it was worth it just seeing that bucket of water fall on their heads," Stephanie said, grinning.

"If you want to get them back, they're in their room — they've been there all night, probably listening to us complain," I said.

Stephanie held up the bucket full of shaving cream and green slime. "Let's throw this at them."

"No — let's wait until tomorrow morning," Kate said. "We can get them in front of everybody."

"Good idea," I said, "since they're always trying to humiliate us in public."

"Not that we don't do a good job of it ourselves," added Lauren.

"Let's think of something really good," Stephanie said.

"Since the room's almost all cleaned up, why don't we try to have a *fun* sleepover," I said. "I'm going to get us some real food. There's a pizza place I saw downtown that delivers up until midnight. I wrote down their number, just in case we might need it. I'll go downstairs and call in our order."

"Double cheese with pepperoni and meatballs," Stephanie called out as I walked toward the door.

"Don't forget the olives!" Kate added.

"And four Dr Peppers!" Lauren yelled.

Sleepover Friends forever!

Even though we were exhausted, we got out to the bus first thing on Monday morning. We had to be there before our roommates.

"So, did everybody have a good time?" Mrs. Mead asked when we checked in with her.

Stephanie gave her suitcase to the bus driver. "Yes and no," she said.

"How about you, Patti? Are you feeling all right?" Mrs. Mead asked.

"I'm just great," I told her. We climbed onto the bus and took our seats. I sat next to Lauren, and Kate and Stephanie sat behind us.

Gradually the bus began to fill up with people. We told everyone that the two seats in front of us were saved. Which they were — for two very important people. We'd noticed Jenny liked to sleep late, so we were pretty sure her group would be the last ones on the bus. The fact that we'd hidden their towels and their toothpaste wouldn't hurt, either.

"I hope this works," Lauren whispered to me.

"It will," I said.

Mrs. Mead was worriedly looking at her watch when Jenny and Angela climbed onto the bus. Ginger and Christy trailed after them. "There are two seats there, and two in the back," Mrs. Mead told them. "Sit down quickly — we need to be on our way."

Angela slid into the window seat in front of Lauren, and Jenny started to sit down in front of me. Just as she did, I reached forward and put something on the seat.

"Aaiiee!" Jenny shrieked, jumping out into the aisle. Angela joined her. They were both staring in horror at the seat.

"Girls, stop fooling around," Mrs. Mead said.

"There's a — a — " Jenny sputtered.

Mrs. Mead walked back and looked around. "Is this all you were screaming about?" She picked up the phony centipede and dangled it in front of them.

Everyone on the bus started laughing. Lauren and I grinned at each other. Success!

"I'll have no practical jokes on this bus," she said. "We need to get home safely. Now, sit down, and we'll get going."

The bus pulled away from the student union,

and Stephanie leaned over the top of our seats. "Hey, do you guys want some gum?" She chomped hers loudly.

"Sure, I'll have some," I said. "Thanks." I took a piece and put it in my mouth. "This tastes really good — what kind is it?"

"Super Spearmint," she said. "Want some, Lauren?"

"Yeah, thanks." She popped a piece in her mouth.

Jenny turned around slowly in her seat. We knew for a fact that she was a real gum-lover. "Do you guys happen to have an extra piece?" she asked, sounding extra polite. She had to know we were steaming mad at her. "I couldn't find my toothpaste this morning, and I had to brush my teeth with just water."

Stephanie counted the pieces in her pack. "Well, I guess I have enough." She handed one to me, and I gave it to Jenny.

"Thanks!" Jenny said. She ripped off the wrapper and shoved it in her mouth. Suddenly her eyes started watering, and she opened her mouth wide, fanning it frantically. She spat the gum back into the wrapper. "Yuck!"

"What's the matter, don't you like it?" I asked sweetly.

She glared at us. "You said it was Super Spearmint."

"It is," said Lauren. "At least, our pieces are." She licked her lips and grinned.

"You must have got the other kind — Super Pepper," Stephanie said. "Whoops!"

Then we all cracked up laughing — all except Jenny, that is.

Sleepover Friends, 1 — Jenny Carlin, 0.

SLEEPOVER FRIENDS

#37 Lauren Saves the Day

Mr. Talbot gave each set of partners in our science class a frog. He explained how to pin the frog down so that we could see its stomach. "I'll do it," Mark volunteered, trying to help me get through it.

Mr. Talbot went on to talk about where to make the incisions, what to look for inside the frog, and how it did or didn't relate to the human body. My head started spinning, and my stomach felt out of control, too. I knew I wouldn't be able to listen much longer without getting sick!

Finally I jumped out of my chair. "I just can't do it!" I cried. I couldn't believe it. Before, I had been afraid of making a scene, and there I was, openly defying a teacher — our brand-new teacher.

SLEEPOVER FRIENDS™
by Susan Saunders

❏ MF40641-8	#1 Patti's Luck	$2.50
❏ MF40642-6	#2 Starring Stephanie!	$2.50
❏ MF40643-4	#3 Kate's Surprise	$2.50
❏ MF40644-2	#4 Patti's New Look	$2.50
❏ MF41336-8	#5 Lauren's Big Mix-Up	$2.50
❏ MF42662-1	Sleepover Friends' Super Sleepover Guide	$2.50
❏ MF42366-5	#16 Kate's Crush	$2.50
❏ MF42367-3	#17 Patti Gets Even	$2.50
❏ MF42814-4	#18 Stephanie and the Magician	$2.50
❏ MF42815-2	#19 The Great Kate	$2.50
❏ MF42816-0	#20 Lauren in the Middle	$2.50
❏ MF42817-9	#21 Starstruck Stephanie	$2.50
❏ MF42818-7	#22 The Trouble with Patti	$2.50
❏ MF42819-5	#23 Kate's Surprise Visitor	$2.50
❏ MF43194-3	#24 Lauren's New Friend	$2.50
❏ MF43193-5	#25 Stephanie and the Wedding	$2.50
❏ MF43192-7	#26 The New Kate	$2.50
❏ MF43190-0	#27 Where's Patti?	$2.50
❏ MF43191-9	#28 Lauren's New Address	$2.50
❏ MF43189-7	#29 Kate the Boss	$2.50
❏ MF43929-4	#30 Big Sister Stephanie	$2.75
❏ MF43928-6	#31 Lauren's After-school Job	$2.75
❏ MF43927-8	#32 A Valentine for Patti!	$2.75
❏ MF43926-X	#33 Lauren's Double Disaster	$2.75

Available wherever you buy books...or use this order form.

Scholastic Inc. P.O. Box 7502, 2931 E. McCarty Street, Jefferson City, MO 65102

Please send me the books I have checked above. I am enclosing $_____

please add $2.00 to cover shipping and handling). Send check or money order—no cash or C.O.D.s please.

Name _____

Address _____

City_____ State/Zip _____

Please allow four to six weeks for delivery. Offer good in U.S.A. only. Sorry, mail orders are not available to residents of Canada. Prices subject to change.

SLE690

THE BABY-SITTERS CLUB®

by Ann M. Martin

Collect Them All!

The seven girls at Stoneybrook Middle School get into all kinds of adventures...with school, boys, and, of course, baby-sitting!

❏ NI43388-1	#1	Kristy's Great Idea	$2.95
❏ NI43513-2	#2	Claudia and the Phantom Phone Calls	$2.95
❏ NI43511-6	#3	The Truth About Stacey	$2.95
❏ NI42498-X	#30	Mary Anne and the Great Romance	$2.95
❏ NI42497-1	#31	Dawn's Wicked Stepsister	$2.95
❏ NI42496-3	#32	Kristy and the Secret of Susan	$2.95
❏ NI42495-5	#33	Claudia and the Great Search	$2.95
❏ NI42494-7	#34	Mary Anne and Too Many Boys	$2.95
❏ NI42508-0	#35	Stacey and the Mystery of Stoneybrook	$2.95
❏ NI43565-5	#36	Jessi's Baby-sitter	$2.95
❏ NI43566-3	#37	Dawn and the Older Boy	$2.95
❏ NI43567-1	#38	Kristy's Mystery Admirer	$2.95
❏ NI43568-X	#39	Poor Mallory!	$2.95
❏ NI44082-9	#40	Claudia and the Middle School Mystery	$2.95
❏ NI43570-1	#41	Mary Anne Versus Logan	$2.95
❏ NI44083-7	#42	Jessi and the Dance School Phantom	$2.95
❏ NI43571-X	#43	Stacey's Revenge	$2.95
❏ NI44240-6		Baby-sitters on Board! Super Special #1	$3.50
❏ NI44239-2		Baby-sitters' Summer Vacation Super Special #2	$3.50
❏ NI43973-1		Baby-sitters' Winter Vacation Super Special #3	$3.50
❏ NI42493-9		Baby-sitters' Island Adventure Super Special #4	$3.50
❏ NI43575-2		California Girls! Super Special #5	$3.50

For a complete listing of all the Baby-sitter Club titles write to:
Customer Service at the address below.

Available wherever you buy books...or use this order form.

Scholastic Inc., P.O. Box 7502, 2931 E. McCarty Street, Jefferson City, MO 65102

Please send me the books I have checked above. I am enclosing $ _____
(please add $2.00 to cover shipping and handling). Send check or money order — no cash or C.O.D.s please.

Name _____

Address _____

City _____ State/Zip _____

Please allow four to six weeks for delivery. Offer good in U.S.A. only. Sorry, mail orders are not available to residents of Canada. Prices subject to change.

BSC790